New Town Ghosts

Mark Rae

It could take four score years or more to work out what
went wrong, and what went right, too. Some say that's
how we get to grow. We are all made of the same three
things, water, love and soul. Music is the thing you feel
without words. When music and words come together,
we call it New Town Soul.

First published in Great Britain 2025
by Mark's Music
49 Errington Road, Ponteland,
Newcastle Upon Tyne, NE20 9LB.

This novel has an accompanying soundtrack, it is available on vinyl
and CD from https://markrae.bandcamp.com, Gardners Books and
Kudos Distribution. It is available on all streaming services.

Typeset by Geoff Fisher

A CIP catalogue record for this book is available
from the British Library.

ISBN 978-1-8384128-3-8

Printed in Great Britain by CPI Group (UK) Ltd, Croydon, CR0 4YY

By the same author

NORTHERN SULPHURIC SOULBOY

THE CATERPILLAR CLUB

This book has an accompanying soundtrack:

New Town Ghosts -
Songs From The Novel By Mark Rae

Available on white vinyl, CD and all streaming sites.

The soundtracks for Northern Sulphuric Soulboy and
The Caterpillar Club are also available to stream.

For Henry

Thanks

Tom Rae - Proof read and Copy Edit

Elizabeth Allen - Copy Editor

Henry James Rae - Artwork & Design

Angie Allgood - Proof read

Paul Arnot - Design

Caitlin Ferrara - Cover Words

Ruth Goodman & Mark Radley at CPI- Production Assistance and Management

Geoff Fisher - Typesetting

Gabriela Bartnik at Sixty Six Productions - Music Manufacturing

The credits for this book's musical soundtrack can be found in the back of the book, along with the lyrics to the songs

1

SIMON HAS A PROBLEM WITH GOD

June 1976, Monday, 8 am, 18 degrees.

The roses in the front garden of the Radcliffe's semi-detached in Kramlin New Town are wilting. A green bottle lays upside down on Simon's bedroom windowsill. Next door's sprinkler creeps lazily back and forth, reminding Simon to brush the stairs. Chores mean more than being responsible in this house.

Simon opens the top drawer of his chest of drawers in the corner of the boxy bedroom and pulls out a pair of thin brown polyester socks. The bottom of the drawer is lined with thick yellow paper adorned with his pencil drawings: fish and crustaceans of the North Sea. Simon is ten and this summer something older than dinosaurs will take over the world. He pushes the drawer and half a conker and a clay pipe with a child's face on the bowl roll into view. Simon keeps important items here in his sock drawer, the things he finds and the things he can't let go.

The pips on the radio signal time for breakfast. Making his way down the stairs to the kitchen, Simon hears the man on the radio say Lincolnshire has called a hosepipe ban and Northumberland could follow soon.

THE SLEEPING BAG

Cracks have started to appear in the open field in front of the Radcliffe's home. The last time it rained in Wellman Way was a Sunday back in May. Simon had looked for a board game to pass the time. Sundays could feel like life was ending. All the shops were closed and TV themes sounded sad. Simon's board games are stored safe under his bed. Casper the Friendly Ghost is his favourite; in the dark the game's pieces glow bright green.

On the last day it had rained, he took his blue sleeping bag from the bottom of his chest of drawers, and dropped the glowing Casper tokens in, then crawled into the polyester tunnel headfirst. Flashes of static sparked against his Admiral England strip and footsteps sounded behind him. Jane, his five-year-old sister had come into the room, her eyelids were stuck together with conjunctivitis.

"Why are your feet sticking out?" asked Jane.

"I'm doing experiments. Go away," Simon replied through the tickly heat of the sleeping bag.

"I do espelimens," lisped Jane, hoping to get involved.

Simon had put Jane in a cardboard box at the top of the stairs during his last experiment, packing the box with cushions and pushing her gently down. It was all going well at first, then the box caught a stair and tumbled. At first it seemed like it was happening in slow motion, then the box raced down the stairs. A cushion flew out and hit the calendar on the wall. The calendar swung back and forth, dropped, then opened on the brown checked carpet at the month of September. There was a short silence, then Jane started crying.

"Is everyone alright?" his mother shouted as the music from Black Beauty played from the lounge on the television. Jane's head appeared from the box, blood dripping from the corners of her mouth, like a face painted for Halloween. Simon stood at the top of the stairs repeating, "She's going to die," and Anne didn't know if she should attend the wounded, or the guilty. A doctor stitched Jane's tongue back together, and Simon had that same feeling he experienced when his mother brushed the stairs, when it should be him doing it.

The air in the sleeping bag was getting old. The polyester held him in its manmade grip.

'Let me teach you,' came a voice in a croaky, high pitch tone and Simon wondered whether it was the voice he had stolen from his sister, or if it was coming from the child's face moulded into the clay pipe he'd found in the farmer's field by the reservoir. The air in the sleeping bag tasted funny, like burnt electricity.

'Who are you?' asked Simon without having to say it loud.

'The girl in the dark,' came the reply.

LET'S GO THROGGING

Saturday morning, 6 am, 17 degrees.

It's the third Saturday in June, the grass in front of the house is yellow and the tap water doesn't taste quite right. Simon pulls on his brown cords and slides a pair of black socks over his milk-white feet. He's getting ready to journey into the empty lands. It's early and the house is silent. Simon creeps down the stairs and turns into the kitchen. The room, the cupboards, the ceiling and walls are bright white and square. The pattern on the Lino floor is complicated and sometimes if Simon squints, he can make things happen inside the distorted shapes. Bright blue sky beams through the kitchen window. Simon picks up a pen and writes, "Off over the railway tracks," on last night's Evening Chronicle and leaves it on the kitchen table. He takes a slice of soft white bread from the plastic bread bin and places it on the chest freezer. Pulling a clean green t-shirt from the washed pile, he slides into it with a wriggle and sits on the step

to slip his black sand shoes on. Carefully he opens the
back door of the utility room, tip toeing across the grey
flagstones and past the vegetable garden. Taking a bite
from the bread he opens the back gate set in the tall,
panelled fence. A pastel green Sprite Alpine caravan is
parked in the driveway, its raised silver logo shining next
to the yellow registration plate. A curved piece of black
rubber sticks out from under the caravan. Simon
wonders if it's an inner tube, like the one inside the
wheels of his Budgie bike. If so, he wants to blow it up
with compressed air and bounce it round the New Town
until he's chased for it. He walks through the small strip
of grass marking the end of the cul de sac and enters the
empty lands with an exhale. Now he's the master, chief
of the newt collectors, champion throgger, sock drawer
stuffer and trainee fisherman. Swatting flies, he crosses
the field opposite the house, ventures over the dual
carriageway to the country lane at the top of the estate.
He crosses the train tracks, walks the bend in the road
where the white walls of the golf club glare through the
plum trees. As he gets closer, he slides into the ditch at
the side of the road, beads of sticky willy attaching to his
clothing. Crawling through the meadow foxtail and
purple loosestrife, he's soon in the car park, faint voices
interchange with the clink of golf clubs and slamming

car doors. He pops up from the ditch and scampers across the car park into cover.

Simon was taught the art of throgging by Paul, an older boy who used to live in the house next door. Paul moved away one day last year, one moment he was playing British Bulldog in the cul de sac, and then he was gone. Something made Simon feel empty after Paul moved, he guessed people must have reasons for going away but they don't share them. Paul had been a good friend to Simon and he knew that with him gone, he would have to navigate the empty lands on his own. Paul taught him the key principle of throgging, to stay on the outskirts of the golf course, far from paths and people. Paul had left him a legacy and it seemed important to Simon that he should pass the skills on. Simon liked helping friends because it was fun and his dad Peter was like that too.

Simon's mind moves quickly, like a squirrel rattling round the branches of a tree. Everything slows down when he draws the pictures in his sock drawer, like his mind was stuck inside a microscope, zooming into the shapes and patterns with deep detail and control. The teachers at Southfield school don't like him drawing in class. They say he should be listening, and he will forget everything that he is supposed to learn. Simon always remembers the things that are important to him, the rules of the empty lands for instance. Where the frog's spawn is going to be and how to take an owl's egg from the roof of a barn. In the empty lands, actions have outcomes that belong to you and you are the one in control.

He weaves through the dense branches of rhododendron at the edges of the golf course until he's in the bushes next to the green of the 14th hole. Over his head, waxy leaves shine; on the ground, dead vegetation crackles in the black dust that seeps through the thin material of his sand shoes. Through a gap in the branches, a golf ball drops from the sky. There's a soft knocking as it bounces, followed by silence, as it rolls across the pristine green. A droplet of sweat runs down Simon's sunburned nose, a second ball arrives and nestles close to the pin.

"You'll never beat me over 18 holes Phillips! Not in a month of Sundays," says the round golfer appearing above the bunker in a garish red jumper and a pair of grey slacks.

"Never is a long time, Jenkins, and I do like a challenge. One day the Brentford Nylons trophy will be resting on my mantelpiece," says the tall and thin golfer in a dark blue jumper, laughing playfully.

"That's if I can find it," says the golfer in red, reaching for his putter.

"Have you lost the company trophy?" asks the golfer in blue.

"I think my daughter might be playing some kind of practical joke."

"They have a strange sense of humour, some kids," says the one in blue, slim body bending to assess the line of the ball to the hole.

Clenching his jaw, Simon bursts out of the bushes and races toward the golf balls sitting pretty like round eggs.

"A rat from the estate!" shouts the golfer in red.

Simon races over the grass, swooping for the double pick up, grasping a ball in each hand, running back to his gap in the bushes and launching himself back into the undergrowth. If Paul was here, he would be proud of this display of throgging, that's until Simon's T shirt catches a branch, snapping it loudly and a jackdaw screeches. The rotund golfer has closed in on him and has Simon by the ankle. He frees himself from the hairy handed grip with a furious leg shake. His sand pump slips off into the golfer's hand. Seizing his chance, Simon dives deeper into the undergrowth, beetles dance across his fingers as he crawls.

"You'll live to regret this rat boy!" shouts the golfer.

Simon threads his way through the undergrowth. Sliding over a crack, he stops, thinking he can hear the voice from the sleeping bag but it's just laughter floating from the golf club. He slips unnoticed through the parking lot and crawls from the hedge onto the backroad. Holding the stolen golf balls tight he limps on one sock past the plum trees on the bend. The warm air is filled with bumble bees droning, greenfly clouding, and the little black flies that get into your mouth and stay until you've no choice but to swallow them.

The tarmac edge is overgrown with dog rose and bitter dock. Standing at the rail crossing, Simon sees the muted grey roofs of the New Town shimmer on the horizon. Back home there'll be Bourbon biscuits sprinkled with sugar and Cornish ice cream in the chest freezer in the utility room.

The smell of creosote welcomes him to the garden fence and reaching for the latch he opens the gate. Concrete paving joins the garage wall running left. Simon's father, Peter, is on his haunches next to the orange garage door. Behind him is his greenhouse, the marrow plants are in flower, yellow petals glow in the sun. Peter is wearing denim shorts and a pair of transparent jelly diving sandals, gold rimmed glasses rest on his strong straight nose, thick swashes of curly black hair shine, and the rules of science sparkle behind his blue eyes. Peter is using a mash hammer and chisel to remove cement from old bricks. Simon chooses not to disturb, and heads for the utility room. Sitting down on the concrete step he takes off his remaining sand pump and pulls the sticky willy baubles from his sock. He takes the golf balls from his pocket with his other hand and rotates the white dimpled surface in his finger and thumb. JP is written in permanent marker on the Titleist ball. He slips them both back into his pocket.

In the kitchen, Simon's mother is sat on a three-legged stool wearing a white dress, her short blonde perm rests on her shoulders, the roots are starting to show, a ski jump nose and green eyes welcome him with a generous gaze filled with concern and, love. Anne is wrapping a bandage around her knee, finishing it off with a safety pin, pursing her lips and inhaling sharply.

"Auntie June is coming over and the stairs and windowsills need dusting, love."

"I was going to --"

"You didn't do it when I asked, love."

"I was...." Simon stops, remembering he doesn't have an excuse.

Simon has been trying to get Jane to do his chores

ever since she started walking. If the box hadn't tumbled down the stairs, he would have asked Jane to 'clean the course for the next run'.

"Don't forget, it's Steven's birthday party tomorrow, and your dad is going to take you all to the cinema," says Anne.

"What are we going to see?"

"The one about the shark, love."

Sharks are older than dinosaurs and it is they that are taking over the world. 1976 is full of them.

Simon runs up the stairs to his bedroom and opens the top drawer of the walnut chest of drawers. He pushes his socks out of the way and rolls the golf balls to the back of the drawer. Next to the trophy.

4

BIG BOY AKA THE FIFTY- SIXER

Friday, 4 pm, 19 degrees.

The Radcliffe family car is a blue Hillman Hunter parked at the bottom of the cul de sac. The plastic covers are still on the seats, making the inside smell of chemicals. Peter talks about buying British, helping people close to home. Working sounds boring to Simon, who would want to do the same thing all the time? Putting food on the table was the answer to those types of questions.

Peter looks big as he turns the ignition key in the Hillman dashboard, the engine starts and the doors vibrate. 'Man to Man' by Hot Chocolate starts to play on the radio. Simon waves at a group of kids on Space Hoppers as they reverse out into the cul de sac, then they pull away and weave through the brand-new curved roads. Rows of box shaped homes pass in ordered perfection. People keep love inside and show it off with tidiness on the outside. Peter turns onto the spine road.

Simon notices the sandstone walls of St Nicholas church, the rows of weather-beaten gravestones alongside. The wind wiped the names off the stone, it seems easy for things to be forgotten. The Hillman pulls up to the big roundabout at the end of the New Town and Simon sees the concrete rim of the local reservoir through the trees.

"How big are the fish in there, dad?"

"I'm not sure there's any fish left in the reservoir, son. Oxygen levels are low, and we need rain for fresh water," says Peter.

"But if there were fish, would they be big?"

"Bigger than the sticklebacks in the stream in the middle of the forest."

Down in Kramlin village there are buildings that look like the church on the spine road. They're building houses in the village too, the old and new don't look so good together. Peter said they were building because new people needed new places to live and there was space here in what Simon calls the empty lands.

Dried mud lies in mounds around the perimeter of the shopping precinct. The path to the supermarket is dotted with saplings, the cycle path alongside, smooth and bike wheels hum when you ride on it. The pebble-dashed wall of the precinct has cherry red lettering on

the side that spells Presto. The supermarket has Top of
The Pops albums lined alongside the tills, girls in bikinis
hold babies on the covers. The New Town gathers like
ants round a sugar cube. Anne buys mince, potatoes,
carrots, fruit, cereal, Lyle's Golden Syrup, and Weetabix
in Presto. Simon makes sure he pushes the cart when
he's forgotten to do his chores, feelings rise up when he's
not doing as he's told and he likes to push them behind
his wall on the inside.

Peter takes the turn for Nelson. Simon's best friend
Steven 'Squeaky' Squire lives in a miner's cottage
opposite the railway station in the old village. Steven
doesn't smile a lot because he smashed his front teeth
out riding a Chopper. The bike was too heavy, he lost
control and fell face first into a kerb. For a while Steven
squeaked when pronouncing words beginning with TH.
You could say Steven looks like a Squeaky now,
nicknames that work like that, stick. Simon first met
Squeaky at nursery school, and even though they are
different, it seems they were sent to each other for a
reason. Friends teach you a lot of things.

Last September, Simon and Squeaky had used team
work to bring down conkers from a chestnut tree on the
back road past the golf course. Simon had climbed the
tree until the thought of getting stuck crept over him,

pinning his mind squirrel the way cats play with their prey. He'd try to calm himself by staring at the sky, hoping to see a sign of the God they'd talked about in school. It was the sight of the slag heap near the center of the New Town that finally brought him back to his senses, he shook the branch while Squeaky continued to throw sticks up at the conkers. Eventually their teamwork brought a cluster down, and inside a fleshy green shell was the biggest conker the boys had ever seen. Squeaky said it was the size of a pony's eye and Simon said they should prove it by holding it next to the pony in the field by the dual carriageway. Simon called the pony over to the barbed wire and held the conker up to the pony's eye, gauging its size by closing one of his own. Being close to the Pony made Simon feel a little strange, in a pleasant way, as if the big eyes of the barrel-chested creature were seeking out the walls he was building on the inside. It seemed silly to connect the two things but the pony understood something about the things that Simon didn't or couldn't yet understand.

The boys bid farewell to the pony, pulling up the last of the clumps of fresh grass out of reach for the pony and dropping them inside the fence. They took their prize conker back to Simon's house, were Peter clamped it in a vice and drilled a hole through the middle. The boys fed a shoelace through the hole and tied a stop knot at one end. They named the conker Big Boy and it performed with great fortitude during school break times, winning fifty-six battles. Then came The Clash of The Long Jump Pit, and everything changed, for good and for bad.

A large angry boy, called Keks, claimed he was in possession of a hundredser and wanted to take on Simon and Squeaky's fifty-sixer. Kek's conker was a cheeser with a flat edge, he'd dried it in an airing cupboard and varnished it. Some of the kids in the playground thought the hundredser was as hard as its owner, but that was plain silly. Keks was hard as a rock, a boy capable of spitting fifteen yards on a still day and picking insects out of the air by their wings.

A circle had gathered to watch the conker clash, swing after swing the fifty-sixer and the hundredser collided. Squeaky attacked skillfully with an inner rage that made his delivery lethal, kids winced like flicked kittens as pieces of conker flew like shrapnel. Simon gave tactical advice, spotting for signs of weakness in Kek's cheeser. The fifty-sixer was holding its own until the strings tangled like laces caught in a mangle, Keks took his opportunity and yanked hard. The fifty-sixer spilled from Squeaky's grasp and rolled out onto the tarmac.

There were gasps, then a lone voice at the back shouted 'Stampsies!' Keks grabbed his opportunity and crushed the fifty-sixer under the metal segs in the soles of his leather bottom Riders. The air filled with the smell of chewed Blackjacks as pupils oohed and aahed. Simon sighed and bent down to pick up the pieces of their beaten fifty-sixer. They'd had a good run but their winning streak was over. He signalled to Squeaky to join him and they slid their backs down the wooden slats of the tuck shop. Simon opened his right palm and gave half of Big Boy to Squeaky; it looked like a little yellow brain, broken down the middle.

Simon thought of Paul next door and how he had flown away like the birds that flew from the oak tree at the bottom of the field when the sun went down. Simon knew that he wouldn't see Paul again. People who move, don't come back.

"Promise me we will always be able to put Big Boy back together," said Simon, looking into Squeaky's twinkly brown eyes. Squeaky took his half of the conker, pressed it into Simon's and they fitted together like two pieces of a jigsaw.

5

LADYBIRDS UP IN THE SKY

Friday evening, 6 pm, 24 degrees.

Older people might think it was unusual that Squeaky would celebrate his birthday like this, with Peter driving them to the cinema in Newcastle. Simon had stopped asking questions about Squeaky's family a while ago. Last summer, Simon asked if his dad ever took him swimming, and Squeaky started crying. Simon wasn't like the other kids who chose to laugh when someone was upset. He just didn't know what to say to make those people feel better. Pain was like the guilt he felt when he hadn't done his chores, it felt better to push that feeling behind the wall inside too.

The lawn in front of the miner's cottage is small, left to go wild like a hedgerow in the empty lands. The faded blue door of the cottage swings open and Squeaky runs across the road to the car. Flared denims flap round his sockless ankles, a bright orange turtleneck clings to his pigeon chest, the bottom tucked into his dark brown elasticated pants. He yanks one of the Hillman's heavy back doors open, jumps on the plastic covered seats, and flashes his crushed raspberry-coloured gums.

"Happy birthday!" say Peter and Simon in unison, Peter's voice deep, Simon's greenstick and willowy.

"Let's go and get Rubba," says Simon.

Rubba lives in a row of new build terraced houses by the Southfield precinct in the middle of the New Town by Alexander Park. His backdoor faces onto a single strip of shops on a steep hill, at the top is a working men's club called The Benny, at the bottom a newsagent, and a chip shop called Fred's Fish. Simon's grandmother works at the chip shop and sometimes gives them scraps of batter that taste of oil. Rubba's real name is Anthony Potts, his nickname comes from his ability to jump off garage rooves and land on his knees. Rubba looks like his nickname too, or maybe people just become what other people call them. Peter said people shouldn't be put in boxes and Simon thought he meant the time he pushed his sister down the stairs and she bit her tongue. Sometimes things get confusing when you're ten, knowing the local lingo helps keep things on track. On the New Town, a plastic bag is made of placka, and a ride on the back of a bike is called a backa. For that reason, Simon's nickname is just Radda, he's jealous of

Rubba's nickname, if you say Rubba Knees once, you'll never forget it.

Rubba is lanky, muscled like a Greyhound, a bowl cut of blonde hair hugs his sharp cheekbones, and his almond brown eyes look like conkers that have been pulled from their shells too early. Rubba loves the hit parade and makes a point of keeping a weekly list of the top ten in the back of his maths book. He's good at whistling, and often switches to a metal contraption called a jaws harp whenever the fancy takes him. Rubba gets Bullet comic delivered by the paper boy every week, The Mice of Tobruk is his favourite strip. Recently Rubba's been saying he knows where his dad keeps a hand grenade, and that he's going to steal it and bring it to the boy's camp under the gorse behind the oak tree opposite Simon's house. Threats like these are normal, the kind you would hear every lunch time on the playground, 'My dad is in the Navy and he's going to shell your house', or 'My dad's a spy and he's going to set fire to your dad's car with a magnifying glass'. Rubba means no harm by it, he just wants to show he can make things happen, the crazier the better. 'Just like the Border Reivers,' he shouts when they're being chased, or when they're the ones chasing. Simon can't remember a time that they chased anyone, they really only chase cats, other boys are dangerous round the edges of the New Town. One November Rubba fired a firework from the top of the slag heap and missed a pregnant woman on the cycle track by an inch. Squeaky said Rubba nearly went to Borstal for that and that he was on a police watch list. Simon didn't know whether Borstal was a place you were taken to or a thing the council did to you. And you couldn't stop them.

Squeaky's favourite comic is called Action, last week the gadgie behind the counter in the newsagents told him it was banned because there was too much blood on the cover. Squeaky said, 'What's a matter with blood, all of us are full of it,' and the gadgie said it was the government's fault. Simon saw a copy of Action at Squeaky's house one time and he was scared to open it past the first page. A shark called Hookjaw was eating people on the cover, sharks had outlived dinosaurs and now they were getting famous for it.

Simon gets Monster Fun delivered every Monday, his comic's shark is called Gums, Simon's grandad Tom has false teeth like Gums but smaller. Grandad Tom comes to sit in the lounge and tutt at the news on a Thursday. He doesn't say a lot, too much of the past has gathered inside his head and overwhelmed him. The stories in Monster Fun help Simon forget about the times he finds

his mother crying at the bottom of the stairs. It happens
when he has spent all day throgging, instead of doing his
chores. Anne has to brush the stairs for visitors when
Simon is out and her knee swells up. Peter told Simon
he was disappointed and the squirrel in Simon's brain
held that word, like a nut, rolled it, then pushed it into a
corner, against the bricks.

The Hillman Hunter is halfway down Gosforth High
Street, the smell of dog pee and chip fat is whistling
through the windows. John Timpson is talking on the
radio; he doesn't sound like people who live on the New
Town.

"The warm weather has seen the harlequin ladybird
arrive in the south of England. The harlequin's shell has
unusual patterns, it's an insect that's known to bite," says
Timpson, as something black thuds against Simon's
wrist, stopping him from riding his arm in the rush of
air outside.

"Can we listen to some music, please?" asks Rubba.

Peter presses the button on the dashboard, the radio
makes a click and the channel changes.

"I wanted to hear about the ladybirds," moans Simon,
looking at the red mark on his wrist.

"There's a reason for the sunshine sky," sing the
Bellamy Brothers. Rubba takes his jaws harp from the

breast pocket of his denim shirt and plucks along in time. Peter leans out of the driver's window, shakes his head, and pulls the car to a halt in a layby. A cow raises its head on the town moor, its black eyes stare like the pony's did.

"I think there's something wrong with the engine," says Peter.

The boys sit in the car with the windows down as Peter raises the bonnet, blocking their view forward.

"I don't want to see Jaws anymore," whispers Rubba.

"Me too, I'm scared it's going to mess with my swimming," says Simon.

Peter drops the bonnet and gets back in.

"I heard the tappets," he says.

"It's just Rubba's harp, dad," says Simon.

"Play it again," Peter turns off the radio.

Rubba plucks the steel tongue and the blue metal flashes in the sunlight.

"That's it! shouts Peter.

They laugh and Peter starts the car.

"Do you know what tappets do, lads?" asks Peter, and Simon sighs. Cars for him mean sickness and torches held still on winter nights.

Squeaky sits forward.

"No Simon's Dad, I don't."

"Tappets are valves that convert the rotation of the camshaft into vertical motion, opening the exhaust valve," says Peter.

"What's a camshaft?" asks Squeaky.

"Can we stop talking about engines, dad, it's making me car sick," says Simon.

"Squeaky is interested, son," says Peter.

"Ok daad," says Simon.

"I want to know, Mr. Simon's dad," says Squeaky.

"Just call me Peter, Steven."

"Just call me Squeaky, even me mam does."

6

JUST WHEN YOU THOUGHT IT WAS SAFE TO GO BACK INTO TOWN

Peter parks the car by the university and they walk down the hill toward the Haymarket. Outside the ABC cinema a crowd lines the ornate facade. A red-haired girl at the front bounces a set of clackers, the balls crack against her wrist, and she starts to cry.

"Stop bubbling man, you haven't even seen the shark yet!" shouts a boy in flared tartan. Morbid excitement builds, Jaws has been out for a year and it's still hunting victims.

Peter leads the boys into the foyer. Simon gawps up at the high ceiling, feeling the plush red carpet under foot. Tickets in hand they leap up the stairs, a skinny man with a waistcoat checks their tickets with a nod. Peter leans on the heavy black door and they're swallowed into the gloom. The smell of stale cigarettes, hot toffee and sweat fills the theatre. Eyes adjust, aisles of red velvet seats curve out, a grey curtain with voluptuous folds guards the screen at the front. The boys find row F and feel their way in the gloom. Peter takes the last spot next to the aisle. On the balcony below, an usher shines a torch on a tray of ices. The curtains slide open, percussion rattles, staccato horns attack, the Pearl & Dean music plays, white shapes zoom in fake 3D from the screen, everyone is falling into the cinematic abyss. The boys stand to dance, shaking off their excitement. A growl of 'get doon' sits them back in their worn velvet seats. Peter sends Simon to the usher with 20 pence, and he returns with four Lyons Maid orange ices and passes them along in the dark.

A short film called Hot Wheels Big Deals starts proceedings. Golden skinned American kids glide across the screen, long hair flowing, riding what the narrator calls skateboards. Zipping around empty swimming pools, they stick to the concrete walls like gravity was a rumour. Simon taps Rubba's knee and they look into each other's eyes, gobs smacked. Simon imagines what it would be like to float over the cycle track, cruising in their version of this four-wheeled American dream. England's weather looks the same right now too, maybe it could all come true? An advert for Keith's caravans reminds them that they live in the empty lands of Northeast England, and not California. The curtains close halfway, then open again to a round of loud oohs. It's time for the angry shark, bottoms tighten, orchestral music swirls, the audience is taken through kelp on the enormous screen. Squeaky grips the ash tray on the arm of his seat and Simon feels like a gulp of American Cream Soda from the pop van is trapped with the other feelings he keeps behind the wall his squirrel sleeps on. He stands up and squeezes past Peter. Squeaky and Rubba get up from their seats and follow, stumbling down the stairs in the dark. Simon sees a dim light above a door, he pushes in and the chipped porcelain of an old urinal greets them. They stand in a circle facing each other.

"We'll have to go back, or your dad will come looking," says Squeaky.

"He's too busy waiting for the shark," says Rubba.

"Just close your eyes when Jaws comes," says Squeaky.

"The music makes it sound like it's always coming, it's a bad monster song," whimpers Rubba, looking green in the exit light.

"One day it might happen to us," says Squeaky.

"You can't even swim," huffs Rubba.

"Try and think about the skateboards, and forget about the shark," says Simon, gripping Squeaky by the shoulders.

The boys creep back into the heat of the theatre and take their seats. On screen, children paddle carelessly in the shallows, Jaws could be close. The boys slip out of their seats, onto the floor. Simon grabs Squeaky's hand. Holding his half of Big Boy, he pushes it into his friend's hand. Squeaky whispers that he didn't bring his half. Simon grits his teeth, staying down behind the seats for as long as he can. Eventually he pokes his head above the seats, Captain Quint is strapping himself into the chair on the deck of the boat. The ratchet of his fishing reel clicks like a Geiger counter. Simon feels sick with fear. Crawling for the aisle he tumbles down the stairs to the toilets, this time, on his own.

Searching for a safe place where the squirrel lives in the branches of his brain, he thinks of the sock drawer in his bedroom. The gold trophy left in their camp under the gorse, the golf balls, the clay pipes from the farmers field, the owl's egg he took from the farmers barn, and the bent bullet from the old firing range at Cresswell. He turns his half of Big Boy in his hand, he can feel the presence of the pony whose eyes were the same size as the conker. He remembers the shadow cast over the rocks in Collywell Bay. He can smell the sea, the music in the cinema rattles the toilet door. He stops the flood of terror by thinking of his mother, her bandaged knee, the tray of tablets by the kettle, the medal on the lounge mantelpiece etched with a woman diving into water. He thinks about Peter, the river Blyth, the power station burning coal that heats up the sea. He thinks about the hedgehog they found by the pond at the back of the golf course and the lice that crawled through its spines. Peter said insects break things down, and that everything goes back into the ground eventually.

'Let me show you,' said the strange scratchy voice in the sleeping bag. Now it was all about what he doesn't want to see, Jaws is reaching a crescendo in the cavernous theatre, walls vibrate and the toilet door rattles even more.

'A watched kettle never boils,' says Anne when Simon is being impatient. The noise stops. He looks at himself in the mirror, he looks white, ghostly. He squeezes his hands into fists, slows his breath, thinks of his English teacher reading poetry, her soft voice making his body tingle. Words can heal if you choose the right ones, in the right order. Simon pushes the toilet door with his foot, the music swirls, the end titles roll, the screen is filled with dark ocean waves. He clambers up the stairs and squeezes into his seat.

"I didn't know that oxygen tanks could explode like that," says Rubba.

"Canny, like," says Squeaky.

"Amazing," says Simon, not knowing if the shark is dead, or alive.

On the street the temperature has dropped and the sky is deep blue. It's light late round here in summer.

"What did you think of the film, boys?" asks Peter, reaching for the handle on the driver's side of the Hillman.

"The first one was best," says Simon.

"It would be cool to have one of those skateboards," says Rubba.

They head for home in the Hillman and Squeaky asks if anyone is up for collecting plums tomorrow. The empty lands call hard on a Saturday. 'Forever and Ever' by Demis Roussos plays on the dashboard radio as the purple lights of the civic center turn on.

"How can we get a skateboard?" says Simon, picking at the plastic covers on the seats.

"I don't think you can get them in England," says Squeaky.

"I remember when all the boys on my street got Davey Crockett hats for Christmas, your grandad couldn't afford one, so he made me a single glove out of a dead badger," says Peter.

"Shh, dad," says Simon.

"Did you know Davey Crockett had three ears?" asks Peter glancing at the row of boys in the back seat.

"No, I didn't, Peter," replies Squeaky and Simon huffs.

"His left ear, his right ear, and the wild frontier," says Peter, dark curls ruffling in the wind of the open window.

"What's a wild frontier?" asks Squeaky and Peter smiles in the mirror.

7

NETTLES IN THE TENT

Saturday morning, 8 am, 21 degrees.

"You've got to do your chores, love, Auntie June is coming round," says Anne, leaning on the three-legged stool by the sink.

"I was going to peel golf balls and make fishing line for sticklebacks."

"You know I struggle with the stairs, love, and your sister is too small."

"She should help as well."

"She does, love, you just don't pay attention."

"There's just so much to do."

"You have growing up to do, love."

Simon picks up the plastic brush and pan from the utility room and heads up the stairs. At the top, a black insect lies upside down on the cream-coloured carpet. He flicks it and it clicks on the gloss paint. Its top side is yellow with black spots. He brushes it into the pan, slides down the stairs and rushes into the kitchen.

"You can't have finished cleaning the stairs, love, you've only been up there for thirty seconds. It takes longer than that to do the job properly."

"It's one of those ones that bite, mum." Simon shows the insect.

"It's a ladybird, love, you didn't kill it?" The smell of soil and fresh water fills the kitchen, Anne stops peeling carrots.

"It was already dead, mum," says Simon.

"If a ladybird lands on you, you'll be lucky," says Anne.

"I want to be lucky and get a skateboard, we saw a film about the kids in America riding them in empty swimming pools before Jaws."

"Your dad might be able to make one, he made bogies when we were young," Anne pulls Simon in for a kiss on the head.

"How long have you known dad?"

"Since we were fourteen."

"That's a long time."

"Some things are meant to be."

"I'm going out to meet Squeaky, I'll be back for my tea but if I'm not, I'll be at Rubba's, in the forest, or over by the train tracks near the golf course," says Simon.

"Don't squash any ladybirds, love," says Anne.

Simon closes the garden gate behind him, the edge of the tarmac in the cul de sac is looking shiny, like the vinyl stacked by the record player in the lounge. The sound of kids playing echoes off grey brick. Simon walks the zig zag path between the estate and the fields to a dual carriageway that marks the end of the New Town. He waits for a break in the cars then sprints across, heading for the railway crossing. Squeaky is leaning against the concrete post on the other side of the tracks; a stem of wheat hangs from his mouth. He's dressed in an orange T-shirt, the neck stretched open like a ghoul's mouth. His brown polyester pants are rolled half-mast.

"Alreet?" asks Squeaky.

"Aye," says Simon.

The boys turn their backs to the New Town and pick up a stick each, slashing at wild carrot and mallow they walk the verge.

"Where's your mamma gone?" sings Squeaky at the top of his lungs.

"Far, far away," Simon joins with the song they sang together at nursery.

On the bend they approach a cluster of trees. Squeaky stops to pull the barbed wire apart.

"Let's get some plums," he whispers.

Simon slips through, holds the wire in return. They

head for the tallest of the plum trees and shimmy up, shifting branch to branch. Clusters of green plums hang in the wilting leaves. Simon reaches for the fattest one and pulls it from the stem. Rubbing it on his sleeve he takes a bite and winces at the bitterness racing from tongue to toe. He turns, shakes his head and they both climb down.

"They're not ready."

"I wanted those," says Squeaky.

"You should have had a sandwich before you came out," says Simon, pulling twigs from his hair.

"My mam didn't leave me anything, my tummy hurts sometimes," says Squeaky.

"You can come to my house for food if you want, just come before we head out," says Simon.

A ladybird lands on Simon's top lip, he brushes it away.

"Who's that?" Squeaky points at a red tent pitched in the dry mud of a layby at the entrance of a farmer's field. They walk toward it, Squeaky kicks a rock and it bounces against one of the guide ropes. The nylon body of the tent flexes, the zip rips open, they glance at each other then turn to run.

"Ahhhhyeeeahh!" comes the ragged cry from behind. Simon looks over his shoulder, three bigger boys in green jumpers with yellow stars are coming. Simon is fast enough to keep distance, the Caramac coloured soles of his sand shoes smacking the rock-hard ground. Squeaky is falling behind, bowlegs buckling, the star jumpers close in on him like hyenas bearing down.

"Aaahhyeeeah," comes the cry again, a claw hammer swinging in the biggest boy's hand. Simon sees the train crossing and the promise of home. He stumbles on a clump of burdock and falls to the ground, turning round to look back as Squeaky screams. Two stocky boys with red hair are forcing him to his knees, yanking him about like hand washing, the tallest of the three raises a hammer over Squeaky's head.

"Get back here ya maggot, or your friend gets nailed," he shouts, voice breaking high to low. With Squeaky, Simon makes one shriveled brain from two pieces of broken conker. If Squeaky is getting hammered, he will have to accept the same fate too. Turning back to face them he walks, panting, head bowed.

"The Seaburn Batlads don't like strangers," says the hammer wielder, voice stuck deep, a mop of lank black hair interrupted by jug ears. His face flat, edges pointed like an anvil, yellow shadows under his eyes, thin pale lips half hiding green tinged teeth set in gums red like squashed berries. His forehead is square like a house brick and a fresh pink scar runs deep through his left eyebrow.

The other two stand either side, almost identical, curly ginger hair raging in the sunlight, two pairs of almond brown eyes squint from their sheet white complexions.

"Who are yee then?" seethes the biggest boy, verdigris teeth flashing.

"Simon."

"I'm Steven," says Squeaky, staring at his feet.

"What's your gang called?" ask the twins in unison.

"Gang?" says Simon.

"Who are yee with?" asks the leader, bringing his lips to a pucker.

"We're from Kramlin," replies Squeaky, tears splattering dust.

"New Town mince, fresh for the stingers. Chig, Arma, shove them in the tent and we'll get to work," says the leader, kissing the claw end of the hammer.

The twins grab them and push them through the zip, arms bent up their backs. The inside smells of hot dog juice drizzled on compost, the sun beats down, the interior glows like torchlight through cheek flesh.

"Chig, Arma, hold them still," says the big one.

A pile of fresh nettles pokes from under a sheet of the

Football Pink, stems cut neatly with a sharp edge. On the ground next to the nettles lies a brass trumpet.

"They call me Lenny, I'm king of the slag heap." Lenny picks up the trumpet, spins it on his finger and holds it in front of his lips, smiling rotten.

"Hold their arms up high," Lenny tells the twins.

"This calls the spirits up." Lenny rubs his index finger up and down the trumpet.

Simon's tongue feels like sandpaper, he taps his foot to hide his shaking legs.

"Do you know how?" Lenny points the trumpet and the hammer at Squeaky.

"No," says Squeaky, sounding like he's dropped a plate of food by the school dinner hatch.

"The heat puts the cracks in the ground," says Arma, pointing his finger at the earth.

"Ghosts need music," says Lenny, looking like Roy Castle trapped in a nylon tent bag.

"Especially the small ones," says Chig, voice squirty like Punch and Judy.

"Little bairns getting buried."

Lenny puts the trumpet to his lips and plays a few notes, it sounds like the song on TV in November, when people dress up in black and pretend to be upset. Simon and Squeaky stare at the hammer, Lenny drops it and the handle stands upright on the plastic ground sheet.

"Who is your fatha?" whispers Lenny in Squeaky's ear.

"Me mam said..."

"It doesn't matter what ya mam said. Sooky needs to know who ya fatha is."

"Who's Sooky?" says Squeaky.

"Shaggy dog stories, never complete, babies buried deep in the old slag heap," says Chig.

"Do you want your story to be complete?" Lenny twirls the hammer.

"No," says Simon.

"Yes" says Squeaky.

"Who smashed your teeth out?"

"No one, I fell off a Chopper."

"Right, pull their pants down," says Lenny lifting the nettles up by their stems. The darkness under the groundsheet crawls with the stinking heat. The Seaburn Batlads are ready to sting the boy's where they shouldn't.

"No!" shouts Simon, ripping his hands from Chig's grasp, he steadies himself before sending a wild punch into the pointed tip of Lenny's Adam's apple. Lenny drops the trumpet, hissing like a mug of tea chucked on a campfire. The nettles land on the twins, Arma squeals like a trapped goat and Simon bursts through the zip, dragging Squeaky behind him. They run for the train tracks, hearts thumping.

"I told you I wouldn't leave you," says Simon, squeezing words between breaths.

"I can't..." Squeaky's legs are like twigs sprayed white for Christmas.

"Just keep running!" shouts Simon.

"I'm paggered, Radda."

"Don't stop,"

They make the railway crossing, red lights flash, the barriers are down, warning that an Inter-City is coming. Simon signals to crouch and they move into a field alongside the railway line. Crawling through cow pats covered in flies, they reach a concrete culvert over a tunnel under the tracks. Simon's mind jumps to the sleeping bag as he enters the tunnel, the voice, and the glowing coins from his Casper the Friendly Ghost game. He reaches for Squeaky, feels his friend's heart beating through his boney fingers.

"We need to wait for them to go," whispers Simon.

"You hit that Lenny hard, Radda, he'll not be playing the trumpet anytime soon."

"I couldn't let them sting us where the babies get

made." Simon tightens his fist, a bruise shows like a memory map fades in.

"If they catch us, they'll kill us." Squeaky holds his head in his hands.

"There won't be a next time, if there is, we can deal with them like we deal with Keks. If we can handle a boy who can spit fifteen yards, we can handle anyone," says Simon.

8

MASH POTATO & BABYCHAM

After the tent incident, 30 degrees.

Coal dust at the bottom of the tunnel's been shaped into pretty rivulets by the last rain. Squeaky picks up the black powder and rubs it between his fingers, they watch it drop through the circle of light at the entrance. The caw of a crow breaks the silence.

"Things aren't good at home," says Squeaky flicking a piece of gravel against the wall.

"Like how?"

"We eat mash potatoes every night," says Squeaky.

"We only get mash potatoes on a Sunday," says Simon.

"We only have Mash Get Smash. My grandad poaches the packets from Presto. My mam's knitted him a jumper with pockets on the inside, to make it easier to lift them," says Squeaky, sniffing off hay fever.

"I'm lucky but my mum's not."

"What's a matter with your mam?"

"Her knee swells, and I have to do chores."

"My mam doesn't do chores, she likes to drink Babycham."

"What's Babycham?"

"Mammy pop, it makes her talk funny. My grandad gave me this last night," Squeaky pulls a piece of brown electrical wire from his pocket, a two-inch loop flops at one end.

"What is it?" says Simon.

"A snare," says Squeaky.

Flicking his finger against the loop, Simon shrugs.

"My grandad said to look for runs and set the snare inside the gap."

"What runs?" says Simon.

"The runs that rabbits use," Squeaky moves back toward the entrance of the tunnel. Simon crawls alongside. Swallows are diving for the flies round the cow pats.

Squeaky exits the tunnel and crouches down the hedgerow. Simon steps up on the culvert and checks the horizon for the Seaburn Batlads. Further down, Squeaky finds a six-inch gap where the long grass is bent to the side a little. He kneels by the run, takes the electrical wire, and wraps one end round a thick branch of hawthorn, pulls it tight and positions the looped noose in the middle of the run.

"Do you think it'll work?" asks Squeaky, face twisted, looking back at Simon.

"I don't know, do you want a rabbit for a pet?"

"The nurse at school said the bones in my legs were growing wrong, it might be rickets. I need to eat more meat and fish,"

"Are your knees going to get swollen, like my mum's?" asks Simon

"Just bent, like Terry McDermott's in the FA Cup final," says Squeaky sniffing.

"Do you have to do housework?" squints Simon.

"My mum doesn't bother with cleaning, they sent people round about it," says Squeaky.

"To do the housework?"

"My grandad said it was the council,"

An Inter-City 125 thunders on the tracks above. Cupping their hands over each other's ears, they close their eyes and scream through the chaos. The sound of the train dies, birdsong returns. Simon looks at the blue tinge on the middle knuckle of his right hand. Fear of the Batlads hurries them down the side of the hedgerow. They arrive at the crossing and wait for the lights to stop and the barriers to lift. The metal creaks, Squeaky squeezes under, out onto the rusted tracks. He pulls a dirty penny from his pocket, lowers himself down and places it on the track.

"Come on man, Squeaky, the Seaburn Batlads could be coming."

"Let's see what happens when a train comes," says Squeaky.

Simon looks beyond Squeaky as the railway line bends into the distance. The Cheviot hills look like someone has painted a piece of cardboard and stuck it on the horizon. People in the Oor Wullie books live up that way and the people who talk on the radio live in the opposite direction. The higgeldy piggeldy routes between each other's houses, the cuts in the cul de sacs, the cycle tracks, the way to school, the chip shop, the newsagent, and the golf course are all that matter to Simon now and that should be enough for anyone to remember.

"It could be hours before the next train comes," says Simon.

"Let's go home then."

"See you at school tomorrow," says Simon as the countryside fades, the zig zag path begins and the patterned brickwork of the New Town swallows them whole.

9

DANCE FOR THE FISHERMAN

Monday morning, 8 am, 22 degrees.

Simon is sitting with his chest compressed between the Formica table and the white radiator on the kitchen wall. He watches Peter kiss Anne and wonders what his dad will be doing at the water works today.

When Simon was four, Peter placed a sugar cube in a teaspoon, added boiling water and together they watched as the sugar cube dissolved. The next morning, Peter showed Simon the teaspoon, the sugar had returned, but it didn't look the same.

"Sixty per cent of the human body is made of water," Peter said.

"Yes, dad," said Simon.

"Factories are polluting our rivers, and it's my job to stop them."

Simon nodded and wondered if the people in charge of the factories would try to stop Peter.

The grey Phillips portable radio delivers the morning

news from the top of the kitchen fridge. For the third day running, the news reader is talking about the cod war, it's been going on for as long as Simon can remember. It's the only war he knows going on between fish and humans, anything can happen beneath the waves.

Last September Simon saw a shore angler with a thick rod on the rocks by Collywell Bay. The fisherman pulled a cod from a gully of kelp, the fish was as long as his sister and covered in light brown spots like the freckles on his arms. Its golden eyes had black centers and its teeth were transparent and glowed like needles made of bone. Simon held Peter's hand as they watched the fisherman guide the cod to the edge of the rocks. The North Sea was coloured black that day, Peter said it was coal dust. Sea coal looked pretty on the beach, like the rivulets in the tunnel under the train tracks, when Simon sat with Squeaky and he told him about the mash potato and being hungry all the time.

The fisherman knelt in the gully in Collywell Bay and slipped his fingers underneath the gills. The cod looked pristine, trapped between worlds, white belly glowing in the rockpool. The fisherman took a six-inch priest from the pouch of his smock and Simon turned to face the cliffs as the crack of bone echoed off behind. A pony on the cliff watched on, black silhouette casting a shadow over them. The cod war must have started right there and then and Simon had seen it begin.

"Does that mean the fish will stop fighting?" Simon asks Anne as the news on the radio changes.

"It means we will stop fighting over fish, love."

"One day I'm going to catch a cod like the man on the rocks in Collywell Bay and I'm going to give it to Squeaky to help to make his legs grow straight," says Simon, sitting on the hallway stairs, tying the laces on his Clark's Commandos.

"But you told me you didn't like what the fisherman did to the fish, love."

"But you said I had to grow,"

"Fish is good for you, love, good for your bones," says Anne.

Simon swings his grey army surplus haversack on his back, exercise books make a hollow sound against his pack lunch box. A quarter cucumber, a cheese sandwich, and a Penguin biscuit are sweating away inside the yellowing Tupperware.

"The following counties are to be added to the hose pipe ban: Essex, Cumbria and Northumberland," says the man on the radio as Simon closes the utility room door.

Simon hears Rubba whistling in the cut between the cul de sacs. Squeaky usually joins them in the corridor by the coat racks. Southfield School is an oblong shape, one-story, built from the same bricks as the New Town. Footballs litter the flat roof, gather in the guttering.

Registration starts, the classes are named after rivers, The Wansbeck, Tweed, Coquet and Blyth. Peter said the river Blyth was running red last night, the second time that week that the Brentford Nylons plant had made a chemical discharge. Simon dreamt he was swimming in the river and couldn't reach the sides.

The teacher calls Coquet class, "Here," come the replies, some kids sound happy, some sad. A bell rings for assembly, black blazers busy like insects. The head teacher Mr. McAdam stands on the raised stage in the hall, head big, body short and round, black suit baggy, white shirt tight, finished with a red bow tie. He greets the flood of sweating children with a hardened stare. Simon watches the tips of the music teacher's brogues as she pushes the pedals on the piano by the gym horse. Simon's mind is wandering already, at school he can make things happen in his head, right now he's reaching into a pond near the 8th hole of the golf course and picking out a greater crested newt. He feels a teacher's eyes boring in and quickly he starts moving his mouth in time with the singing.

"I danced for the fisherman, for James and John. They came with me, and the dance went on. Dance, dance, wherever you may be, I am the lord of the dance said he."

The singing stops, the sun beats down through the high windows. The headmaster is talking about God, Simon knows God has a beard and a pointed finger. Peter doesn't go to church, he believes in science, Anne is a Methodist, which sounds like science. Anne said Peter's love of science saved him, like religion gave people purpose.

Simon wonders, where does all the love that people send to God go? Does it pile like the spoil on the slag heap in the middle of the New Town. He wants to know why the love he sends doesn't stop his mother's knees from swelling. Couldn't God clean the stairs at home with wind? He must know Simon doesn't like doing chores. Why didn't God stop the cod war? There'd been an assembly about Jesus last week. The headmaster said Jesus had fed thousands of families with small fish, they must have been sticklebacks, thought Simon. Then the headmaster said Jesus had gone fishing for men, maybe Simon could fish for different Gods? A God of Legs would be good. With a God like that Simon would know where the love he sends goes. The God of Legs could help his mother and Squeaky. Rubba could get a job as a saint, jumping off garages on to your knees is a hard skill to master. Even Jesus couldn't do that.

Simon's mind is moving fast, his squirrel is flying through the branches. A man called Cliff Richard had been singing about a devil woman on the radio in the kitchen last week. Why write a song about the devil? It seemed risky, unless people were making the stories up and changing them to suit what they wanted. A boy called Kenneth had moved to the school a few months back and he promised everyone a catapult and a bag of steelies. As the weeks went by, there were still no sign of the presents he'd promised. For a while, Kenneth said his dad couldn't get them down from the loft because they were too big. Eventually Simon thought he was just trying to make new friends in a new place. It's OK to feel alone when things change, and to want things another way.

Simon's staring at an ant now, watching it wind across the plastic tiles, it looks like his slower thoughts, when the squirrel sits still when he's fishing or roaming the empty lands. Simon is dreaming of the summer holidays; he imagines riding a skateboard like the kids before Jaws. The rush of warm air against his skin, the hum of wheels on the smooth cycle track, when six weeks feels longer than a year. The images of freedom hang like nana's perfume in the lounge. The assembly ends and the daydreaming crashes into reality. Like a cheap army, the children shuffle out into the corridors, gangly and part formed. Simon notices the back of Rubba's blazer is shiny.

"Someone's been gobbing on you," he whispers.

Rubba takes his blazer off and turns it around. Keks is looming like a hate moon; he's grown a few inches taller since Big Boy got stamped in The Battle of The Long Jump Pit. Keks' body is pushing at the seams of his uniform, his grey eyes are filled with ill will, and bum fluff furs the chin of his turnip shaped face. Waiting to turn black.

"What yee lookin' at?" hisses Keks, spit glowing with the dust floating in a beam of sunlight, his lips stained yellow with Smith's Horror Bag crisps.

"Nothing," replies Rubba, who continues to whistle "Combine Harvester", like a stovetop kettle coming to the boil. The clarity of Rubba's whistling is enough to confuse Keks, who turns round and punches a boy hanging his blazer on the back of the head instead. Seizing the opportunity to escape, Simon and Rubba run down the corridor to the open sky of the playground, hunkering down against the wooden slats of the tuck shop.

"Me and Squeaky set a snare by the golf course, he's trying to catch a rabbit to eat with mash potato, so his legs can grow straight," Simon explains as Rubba opens a fruit salad, squinting into the light.

"We got chased by radgies up by the golf course, they were going to sting our privates with nettles, one's got a trumpet that brings ghosts up from the cracks in the ground." Simon holds his right hand out, the bruise is gooseberry green now.

"I punched him on the neck, then we ran and crawled into the tunnel under the railway track. Squeaky set a snare along the hedgerow when the coast was clear."

"Are they after us?"

"I reckon," says Simon as the whistle blows, ending breaktime. The dinner nanny rounds up the stragglers. Simon and Rubba jog to the double doors and head down the corridor to classroom 3B. It's time for Religious Education.

10

CHEESY RICKETS

Tuesday, 11 am, 23 degrees.

Mr. Temperton is standing at the front of the class in a shiny brown suit, a wide cream tie hangs from his neck like a dead flatfish, grey sideburns creep across his cheeks like weeds and his teeth look like sweetcorn has been spilled onto crepe paper. God must love him.

Mr. Temperton picks up a thick black book from the wooden table at the front and starts reading. Simon's stomach sinks, the teacher's voice sounds like air from a month of wet Sundays has been forced into a bagpipe and squeezed out half-heartedly.

"Book of Exodus Chapter 10 verses 12-15. The locusts covered all the ground until it was black. They devoured everything, nothing remained green in all of Egypt."

The finger-pointing God only seems to like hot countries, thinks Simon. The God of Legs could be like one of the Viking Gods and visit cold countries. It seems obvious that Gods should work where they are needed most. Simon's seen people going into the church on the spine road, all dressed up and tottering with repentance. He's also seen people singing close to candles during Songs of Praise on TV. All that love and attention is given to the God who doesn't show up much. Simon thinks about what he needs to do for the God of Legs to start working. An altar would be a start. He remembers the Action Man that lost its head during one of his experiments in the back garden. The plastic legs could be the altar, or maybe he could make a female God of Legs with one of his sister's dolls. Female gods would do a better job, boys forget to do their chores, sometimes it feels like they forget to do the right thing on purpose.

Simon's thoughts jump to last Summer, a week when all his friends were away. He had tried to get to the reservoir to catch fish but he couldn't get through the fence. Instead, he decided to venture into the field alongside the reservoir. The wheat in the middle of the field had been flattened into the shape of a circle. He laid there on his back and stared at the sky. Simon felt emptiness, a sense that he himself was just a moment, and that nothingness was drawing him slowly back into the cracks in the ground. Lenny said there were ghosts in there and Simon wanted to forget that he'd ever met

Lenny or the Seaburn Batlads. He knew that the
nothingness was part of who he was inside, down in his
soul, and that he should accept it for what it was. He
knew that the New Town had been built to forget things
too, that's why the buildings looked different next to
each other.

A kid called Robson puts his arm up at the front of
the class.

"Is Egypt far away, sir?"

"It's in the Middle East," says Mr. Temperton.

"By Nottingham, sir?" asks Slack, squinting through
his NHS glasses, eyes like black bullets in the bottom of a
pint glass. Keks snorts, even the school hooligan knows
Egypt is further south than Nottingham, by two hundred
miles at least. Mr. Temperton turns his back to draw the
outline of a locust, a battery of rulers are loaded with
chewed paper and the soggy ammunition is fired at
Slack. The back of Slack's head is peppered like the first
snowflakes landing on a slate roof. Slack wipes his hand
down the back of his head and growls.

"Quiet!" shouts Mr. Temperton, turning round, face
knotted. He gathers his anger into a shiver and
continues.

"Now then, who has heard of the Pyramids?"

All the hands go up, apart from Simon and Squeaky.

"Radcliffe, Squire, will you stop looking out of the window. For the love of God, what's out there?"

"Rabbits, sir," says Squeaky.

Mr. Temperton walks over to the boys and looks out of the window. Mr. Blenkinsop, the school PE teacher, is on the football pitch, hitting mole hills with a sand tamper, his moustache like a yard brush buttoned to his lip.

"If you think rabbits are more important than God, you can get out of my class! Stand in the corridor, you mini plagues of ignorance," Mr. Temperton points at the door and his dead fish cream tie pops out of his brown suit blazer.

The boys pick up their bags and leave the classroom. They stand outside, backs against the wall.

"You won't tell any teachers about the snare, will you?" says Simon, bouncing his back off the scuffed paintwork.

"They will say we are living like wild animals, and we'll get chucked from school."

"The social services were talking to me mam in the kitchen last week and she was bubbling," says Squeaky.

"You can have my food, you know?" says Simon, tapping on the Tupperware box in his bag.

The dinner bell rings. Religious Education ends, the

door swings open and the children run from God. The stampede bursts into the dining room. Simon captures an empty table near the door, throwing his haversack across the fake wood finish. They sit and break open their pack lunches. Squeaky has a Presto bag with a slice of white bread crumpled up inside. Simon snaps his Penguin biscuit in half and hands a half to Squeaky.

"Two pieces, like Big Boy."

Mrs. Shields, the dinner lady watches on in her white pinny, hair dyed blue, skin wrinkly like the tripe you see in the white plastic tray at the butchers. She comes over, tuts, and leaves a cheese scone next to Squeaky.

"Is cheese good for rickets?" whispers Squeaky.

"It's easier to catch than rabbits, your grandad could get some at Presto," says Simon, tapping Squeaky's foot under the table.

Brassa, the spoon controller, a kid with curly blonde hair and buck teeth approaches the table, he rubs his belly in front of Squeaky and laughs. Rubba stops whistling 'Silly Love Songs' and jumps up from his chair to flick Brassa on the forehead with the back of a fork. The metallic clunk rings through the dinner hall, drawing the blue rinse battleship back to the table.

"If there's any more shenanigans from you worky tickets, I'll send you to the headmaster's office for the cane!" growls the dinner lady. Rubba and Brassa let go of each other's lapels. Simon and Squeaky's eyes glaze over, the sugar from the Penguin biscuit rushes through their veins.

Lunch break ends, pupils file into the cramped corridors. Simon sees a piece of long hair hanging from Squeaky's trouser pocket. It must be from last week's fight between those girls. It started on the playground and snaked its way down the cycle path. Sandra Phillips and Becky Jenkins wanted to yank the hair from each other's scalps.

"I would never steal a naffing trophy from your place," Becky had shouted, before taking flight down a cut between the houses. Squeaky had picked up some of the hair torn out during the fight. A memento of 'how to win dirty' said Rubba, an essential skill in any battle, he reckoned. Rubba would use these moments to tell everyone that his dad used to be in the army. Simon wondered if the trophy he found in the gorse camp and kept in his sock drawer might be the same one. Whatever came of it all, it was his, for now.

11

THE INDUSTRIAL REVOLUTION

Wednesday, 10:30 am, 24 degrees.

Classroom 4 F, second lesson of the day. Mr. Tebbins is stood at the front of the class in tweed pants, a musty yellow blazer, his face folded in on itself like tossed semolina. A rumour has spread that Mr. Tebbins keeps a baby crow in his pocket, on account of the screeching that follows him up and down the aisles. Others say he was in a car crash and that he has steel toes at the end of his shoes. Mr. Tebbins teaches history and looks old enough to know about the stories firsthand. The Industrial Revolution is written in chalk at the top of the blackboard, a hastily drawn map of Northumberland sits underneath it, in the middle, Kramlin is pinpointed with an arrow. Mr. Tebbins scrapes 'YOU ARE HERE' and starts drawing what looks like gallows around the New Town. The chalk scrapes. Simon grits his teeth.

"Does anybody know what these are?" the teacher asks.

Hands reach up, Tomma at the back gets picked.

"Is it hangman, sir?"

"No, Thompson. Has anyone in the class heard the phrase, 'Like taking coal to Newcastle'?"

"The toon sir?" asks Slack.

"Yes, four eyes! Only a fool would take coal to Newcastle. And why would that be?" Mr. Tebbins scans for interest.

"Because it's heavy, sir," says Simon.

"No, Radcliffe, you wouldn't carry coal to Newcastle, because there's no need to, you're sat on top of it," Mr. Tebbins strides between the pupil's desks, the metal crow screeching in his toes, chest stuck out like a puffin on Marsden Rock, his thumbs tucked tightly into his grease-stained lapels. He stops next to Simon's desk and starts booming.

"It's everywhere, under the fields and hills, out there under the sea. The slag heap you all sledge down was made from the spoil dug in search of black gold, the very material that fired the industrial revolution!" Mr. Tebbins punches his palm, it sounds like bums being smacked. He walks slowly back to the front of the class.

"The year is 1862, down Hester Pit, over New Hartley but a mile from here. Miners trapped with their children, poison gas seeping through cracks, rising water and collapsing seams," Mr. Tebbins makes a circle between the arrow that marks Kramlin and the coast at Seaton Sluice.

"You will be paying a visit to the memorial, soon."

Simon remembers the last time it rained, he was upside down in the sleeping bag, the taste of stale air and nylon static, before the voice came. He puts up his hand.

"Yes, Radcliffe," says Mr. Tebbins.

"Sir, did they get out?" asks Simon.

"You can wait for the trip, Radcliffe," says Mr. Tebbins, flashing an unpleasant smile.

A sheet of paper is handed out. The words are set like the hymns Simon mouths in assembly.

"The Hartley Calamity by Joseph Skipsey. All read with me," says Mr. Tebbins.

"Oh father, 'til the shaft is rid,
Close, close beside me keep,
My eyelids are together glued,
And I-and I must sleep."

The children's voices are all jumbled. Mr. Tebbins stops, walks over to the windows, drops the blinds, and pulls the blue curtains together. The classroom falls dark, stuffy.

"Radcliffe, what are you scared of?"

"Me sir?" says Simon, still thinking of the voice in his head that came to him on the last day it rained.

"Yes, you Radcliffe, are you not listening boy? What are you scared of?"

"Sharks, sir," says Simon.

"Been to see that silly little film?" Mr. Tebbins tuts.

"Jaws ate a lot of people, sir," says Simon holding his hands in tight fists beneath the desk.

"He hid in the toilets for most of it," says Squeaky, the class bursts into laughter, then collectively remembers, insolence equals caning, silence returns, quickly.

"There aren't any sharks in the North Sea, Radcliffe. You just like feeling scared," says Mr. Tebbins. Simon shakes his head, anger rising from behind his wall; a twig from the empty lands falls from his hair into the ink well in his desk.

"There are sharks in the North Sea, sir, off the hot water pipe by Blyth power station. My uncle says they come in after the mackerel at the end of the Summer," says Rubba.

"Codswallop, Potts, your uncle is a liar. Squire, tell me, what are you scared of?"

"Ghosts and being hungry sir," says Squeaky. The class titters.

65

"Stop laughing you little oxygen thieves. Can you imagine what it would be like to spend every day in the dark?" Mr. Tebbins booms maniacally.

"No, sir," mumbles Skillet at the front, touching his perfectly knotted school tie. Mr. Tebbins pulls the curtains back, light floods squinting eyes.

"Class dismissed."

Simon, Squeaky and Rubba join the throng of blazers filtering through the bottle neck of the school gates. It's 3:15, everyone's favourite time of day.

"Are you coming to check the snare, Rubba?" asks Simon.

"I can't, me mam wants us straight back for me tea," says Rubba.

"Are you scared of what I told you by the tuck shop?"

"About what?"

"About the Seaburn Batlads?" asks Simon.

"Nah, it's me mam, she likes to make sure I have a good tea inside me."

"See you tomorrow Rubba," says Squeaky.

12

LEVERATED SPIRITS

Sunday, 10 am, 25 degrees.

Simon and Squeaky walk the smooth grey tarmac of the cycle path, past the cul de sac where Becky the scalp tugger lives, down the zig zag path, along the trees that hide the stream in Stickleback Forest, across the dual carriageway, down the back road to the train crossing. Squeaky bends down to look between the tracks and picks up the penny flattened by the Inter City 125.

"My grandad said to keep clear of the tracks or I'll end up locked up like great uncle Sam," says Squeaky.

"To scare you off them, right?"

"A train crashed, and Sam got sent to prison for it,"

"He crashed a train?"

"It was The Flying Scotsman."

"I tried to draw the engine on that train once, the steam was the hardest bit."

"Uncle Sam was trying to get more pay for working

down the pit. Grandad says the owners won't let you stick up for yourself."

"Can I see?" Simon holds his hand out and Squeaky drops the penny in his palm.

"You can't see the Queen," says Squeaky

"Wiped flat."

They turn their attention to the snare and walk the hedgerow lining the bottom of the tracks. Squeaky slows. Recognizing the rabbit run, he gets small and brings his finger to his lips. There's a scuffling sound, a furry shape darts between the branches of the hedgerow.

"It worked!" Squeaky pulls back the tangled stems of bladder campion, a furry brown object cowers at the end of the electrical wire.

"It's a rat," warns Simon.

"It looks like a rabbit," says Squeaky.

"We should let it go you know, it's just a baby," says Simon.

"My mam wants dinner, go on, get it, please."

"Why me?" quizzes Simon, looking down at Squeaky's bowlegs.

"Cos your dad helped you be good at things."

"Keep an eye out for the Seaburn Batlads."

Simon crawls in, the rabbit darts, yanked to a standstill by the wire.

"Slow down little one," Simon whispers, pinning the bundle down as he loosens the snare. He feels a sickness, a pain near his heart squeezing guilt bubbles pressed against the wall his squirrel sleeps on. He stops the water bulging up in his eyes and reminds himself that Squeaky is hungry, his legs are going to get more bendy and things aren't good at home. He prays to the God of Legs that this won't start a new war, like the cod one on the radio. He backs out of the run, the trembling creature cupped in his palms. Squeaky opens the side pocket of Simon's green parker and Simon guides it in on top of the Spangles wrappers and biscuit crumbs.

"Let's go home with it," says Squeaky.

"Is your dad a radgie gadgie?" asks Simon, thinking of the hiding they might get for bringing a live animal back, instead of a dead one.

"I have a grandad, and me mam," says Squeaky.

"Is that why you like to listen to my dad when he talks about engines?" Simon pats his pocket gently, the warm lump moving like a joey kangaroo in its mum's pouch.

"What do you mean?" replies Squeaky.

"It's OK if you like my dad, is all..."

"I don't want to talk about those things," says Squeaky.

The boys walk the grey tarmac of the cycle path, cross

over the dual carriageway, and stop on the raised grass of the roundabout before the sandstone buildings of the old village start. In the distance, people file in and out of Presto. A stray shopping cart lays on its side on the verge. Simon rights it and Squeaky jumps in. They rattle over the road, back on to the smooth surface of the cycle track and on to the miner's cottages by the station. Brenda greets them at the door in a green and yellow star jumper. Her face pale and crinkly, her hair the colour of straw.

"We caught something to eat, mam," says Squeaky.

"Aye, and what is it?" Brenda exhales smoke into their faces. Simon coughs and blows some away.

"Have a look in Radda's pocket, mam," says Squeaky, puffing his pigeon chest out. Simon undoes the buttons on his parka and pulls it open. Brenda leans in, smelling of fruit and fire, like the air that drifts from The Bay Horse Inn when they walk past on their way to the Tarza swing by the spine road.

"Eeh, well, you couldn't even get half a sandwich out of it!" she shrieks, stubbing her cigarette out on the wall and flicking it into the front garden, where it joins a pile.

"Does that mean we have to have Mash Get Smash for tea again?" Squeaky's eyes roll.

"Your grandad's lifted mince from Presto," says Brenda.

"We're going to have mince!" shouts Squeaky, bursting in through the living room, past the brass horseshoes hanging over the fireplace, and on to the cupboard kitchen. Simon follows, watching as Squeaky pushes bottles aside in the fridge, the Babycham clinks as he stares at the wrap of mince like it was a satchel of gold.

"Be quiet, your grandad's asleep in the garden. You can let that rabbit go, Radda," says Brenda.

Simon notices her teeth are a dark yellow, with a hint of green. He nods.

"Nee worries. I can hear it all, send the lad and his marra through," comes the gravelly rolling r's of the Northumbrian brogue from the garden. Squeaky and Simon walk into the wild weeds. Grandad Joe is laid out horizontal in a deck chair, dressed in a string vest, camouflage trousers, a pair of red braces and a snot rag knotted on his nappa.

"We set the snare, grandad."

"Aye, and what did you fetch?"

"A baby rabbit," says Simon pulling it from his pocket.

"That's no rabbit, she's not for the pot. I'll take you

boys out lamping proper, sometime soon, before the council come back," says Joe.

"Not in front of the bairn," says Brenda, lighting another coffin nail.

"I'm off home, Squeaky, I'll see you at school," says Simon.

"Let her go in the big field, bonny lad. She's a leveret and you don't want the spirits," says Joe.

"Spirits?" replies Simon.

Joe winks.

"Aye bonny lad,"

Simon has seen Peter use methylated spirits to clean metal in the garage, Joe can't mean that smelly liquid, surely? Even if you crushed a hundred rabbits you wouldn't get purple out. He closes the flap of his parka pocket and heads through the grey smoke-filled fug of the cottage and sets for home. It's close to 6 pm, the smell of two-stroke petrol drifts with the sound of lawn mowers. 'Summer in The City' by The Lovin' Spoonful plays on the radio in the garage as Anne greets him in the utility room.

"Have you had fun, love?"

"I've got something to show you, mum." Simon pulls open his pocket and lifts out the fluffy bundle. Anne sees the graze the snare made on its neck, she pulls cotton wool from a drawer and runs it under the hot tap. Simon holds it still as Anne cleans the creature's neck. Jane walks into the kitchen in her nightie, half asleep.

"Show me," Jane says.

Simon lifts it out of the sink, velvet ears brushing the bruise on his hand.

"It's withch," lisps Jane, the hem of her nightie hovering, like she's floating.

"The anti-biotics are giving your sister nightmares, love. Go and ask your dad for a box," says Anne.

"I am going to call her Tiny," says Simon, carrying the living bundle down the flagstones to the garage door. 'Young Hearts Run Free' plays loud, the bare bricked interior of the garage smells of rust and oil. A mechanic's light is clamped to the open bonnet. Hack saws, hammers, and a diving suit hang down from a row of six-inch nails poking from the brickwork. The front of the car is jacked, Peter's oily jeans stick out like he's been knocked down by his own car.

"Dad, I need a box for a pet," shouts Simon over the radio.

Peter wheels himself out on a trolley.

"I've been fixing the tappets, son, what's this then?" His gold rimmed glasses sparkle in the lamp light.

"Squeaky wanted to eat it but his mum said it wasn't big enough," says Simon.

"How did you manage to catch it?'

"We snared it. Squeaky's grandad Joe told him how to do it, he said it was a leveret," says Simon.

"Joe the poacher fixed a fox problem at the water works for me a while back. The skull is on your shelf. You're lucky you didn't catch a badger, that would've been a different kettle of fish, son," says Peter, making a claw with an oily hand.

"I don't think Squeaky's got a dad, he says his mum drinks Babycham and they eat mash potatoes every night," says Simon.

"For Mash get Smash," Peter sings the jingle Simon's heard on the television as he reaches up to a shelf with stacked cardboard boxes.

"I've been giving Squeaky food at school, he says his tummy hurts," says Simon propping himself against the wall.

"That's good, son, but that should be a matter for the social services.,"

"Is that the council?" The leveret's eyes look like black marbles.

"The people we pay taxes to are supposed to protect the vulnerable. Here, this box should work. And a leveret is a young hare, son," says Peter.

"What's the difference between a rabbit and a hare?"

"Hares have bigger ears and live in pairs, like your parents. Rabbits live in large groups called droves."

Simon lowers Tiny into the box.

"Thanks, dad."

"I'll make a hutch for Tiny tonight. I've got to get the engine fixed for the weekend, first," says Peter, sliding himself back under the car.

Simon stops and picks fresh lettuce from the vegetable garden. Anne takes the box in the utility room and lowers in a bowl of water. Peter comes in from the garage and washes his hands, scooping a lump from a jar marked Swarfega. The green slime sparkles as it drips into the sink.

"Let's go for a ride, test these tappets."

Peter and Simon get in the Hillman and drive the back lanes over the train tracks, the tires judder in the dips where Squeaky left the penny. Simon doesn't mention what happened in the tent as they drive past the entrance to the field. Talking could steal freedoms, getting banned from the empty lands is not an option.

The trees arc over the lane, sun light flashes through the leaves like the cine film Peter projects onto the lounge wall. Simon sees three boys bending over a sapling in a clearing, one is wearing a green jumper with yellow stars. Simon's squirrel jumps to the history lesson, and the children in New Hartley.

"Can children live underground, dad?"

"Why do you ask, son?"

"The teacher said miners and their children were trapped in New Hartley."

"Life was cheap."

"Is it still cheap now?"

"The rivers will be next, son,"

Simon looks across at his dad's hands gripping the black steering wheel. Water changes things.

The forest fizzles away to waste land, Peter pulls up by a roadside dump. A white-tailed deer grazes by a rusted engine block, lifting its head and bolting. Simon looks down into the ditch, bright green caterpillars are crawling across fruit crates. Heaving the passenger door open, he notices blisters in the paint by the handles. In the winter Peter will sand them down and paint over them.

"Pick the crates up, son, we'll make them useful again," says Peter.

Simon jumps down into the ditch and pushes the honeysuckle aside. He pulls the crates out and hands them up. The key turns, the car coughs into life and they head back to the New Town. Simon turns his head to look through the rear windscreen. Three figures appear in the dust, yellow stars on jumpers.

"Go faster, please, dad," says Simon, feeling sick as they hit the curve in the road by the plum trees.

13

STICKLEBACK FOREST

Sunday, 10 am, 24 degrees.

Peter is pulling bricks from a stack against the garage wall. Anne sits on a block of driftwood, darning a pair of Simon's socks.

"The nurse at school said Squeaky needs to eat fish to stop his legs bending," says Simon.

"We need vitamins, for our bones, love," says Anne.

"Have you got rickets?" Simon looks at his mum through his seaside fishing net.

"No, love, I've got rheumatoid arthritis."

"When will it go away?"

"Just help with the chores, love."

"How do you get rooma, what's it called?"

"Rheumatoid arthritis," Peter repeats, so Simon doesn't forget.

"Having babies."

"Was it me or Jane?"

"Don't be silly, love, it happened before you came along."

"So, a baby we don't know was here before us?"

"Don't be silly, love."

"I'm going to help cure Squeaky's legs. Last week Keks was teasing him, and he cried. Keks said he couldn't stop a pig in a passage."

"Little blighter," says Peter, lifting a roll of bitumen felt onto the new hutch.

"He's the biggest boy in school, dad."

"The bigger they are, the quicker they cry, son."

"That sounds hopeful. I hope we can get Squeaky some fish to eat before the pig turns up," says Simon, staring at Peter's hammer. It's bigger than the one Lenny from the Batlads swung.

"Your new pet will be in here by tonight."

"Thank you, dad, you know how things work. I'm off down the stream, to get some sticklebacks."

"We played in bombed out houses, at your age, son."

"That sounds like fun."

Simon opens the back garden gate and heads over the yellowed field in front of the house. In the distance the top of the hedgerow is broken by elders marking the water line. The elders lead to Stickleback Forest, a place where oaks and sycamores reach up to the sky and garlic mustard rolls a fragrant carpet on the ground. The stream is deepest in the middle of the forest. Simon is wearing his nylon Wombles T-shirt, Orinoco stares out from his chest, Tobermory peeks from under his armpit. He stops on the mud bank and pushes aside the white flowers of arrowhead. Turning over a half-buried house brick, he grabs a lobworm as it pulls back into the ground. The worm snaps, leaving one half writhing in his hand. He takes his burgundy pen knife and the golf ball marked JP from his pocket and peels the shiny white surface off with the blade. The elastic core on the inside looks like a miniature ball of wool. He pulls the elastic and ties the end to the worm. In the stillness, Simon can feel his mind squirrel slowing, random thoughts disappear like the sky melting into black when the sun falls off the earth.

Two fat sticklebacks sit in midwater, their bodies sparkle silver. Simon pushes his net into the soft mud and the fish dart under a stone. He throws the worm into the water, pulling the elastic until it wriggles over the net. Time made forests, and fish are soon to forget, electric blue eyes hover, shifting closer to the trap. Simon thrusts the net up and a wood pigeon cracks its wings. A stickleback tosses against the rainbow pattern in the mesh.

'Remember me son?' The s spits like an adder under foot. It's the high scratchy voice that came to him in the sleeping bag on the last day it rained.

"Get away," hisses Simon.

'It's too late,' says the voice.

"Who are you?!" shouts Simon as Squeaky's grandad Joe passes on the bank. Simon can feel himself turning the colour of the stickleback's belly.

"Are ya alreet, bonny lad?" asks Joe, staring at the inch-long silver and red quarry, flipping in Simon's net.

"I'm after Rodney red bellies."

"If you want big fish, you've got to think like one, we'll go ticklin' with Steven before the council come back," says Joe, spitting a wheat stem. Simon turns the net over, the fish falls on the bank, dust blackens its body. He helps it back in and it darts away like Joe, melting into the forest. Simon picks up his net and heads for home.

He kicks off his wellies in the utility room.

"We've got something to tell you," Anne supports her weight on the kitchen table.

"Probably shock, son," says Peter rubbing his chin at the door.

"What shock?" says Simon, eyes darting.

"It's Tiny," says Peter, putting his arm around his shoulder.

Simon kneels by the hutch, moves the straw, Tiny's eyes are wide open, still. She looks different, like the sugar cube that changed in hot water.

"Come on, son."

Peter takes a spade from the garage, and they walk across the field in front of the house in silence. Jane follows behind, holding lollypop sticks tied together in a cross. At the base of the oak tree, Simon holds the limp body and Peter digs a hole. The leveret feels cold in the heat as the spade bounces off the hard ground. Simon thinks of the spirits Joe mentioned, then how Jane said the leveret was a witch. 'God of Legs if you are listening,' whispers Simon in his head, 'Squeaky needed food, and it wasn't my fault.'

Even the cracks in the ground didn't help with the digging of the hole. Peter drove the spade hard into the parched earth. Simon thought about how long it would take to dig a mine. Peter took the leveret and placing her body in the hole, Simon felt the sickness inside spread and grow, inviting fear behind the wall. If hares live in pairs, like mums and dads do, would Tiny's partner come here too? The thought felt like a scab picked too soon. The child's face on the clay pipe came from the farmer's field. The past hides stories, not all of them get told.

That night, Simon dreamt that Tiny was trapped in a ball of electrical wire in the drainage tunnel by the train tracks. He was cleaning its neck with a hairbrush and

Jane watched on, whispering 'witchth' until it sounded like an inner tube inflating. The leveret's fur sparkled like fry gathering to shoal. The light in the tunnel was fading. Simon saw Squeaky's shadow, a cloud of ladybirds blocked the light, the rush of metal-on-metal tore through the air like a haunting. Simon and Squeaky were facing each other, screaming over the Inter-City, hands over ears, tentacles of sound crawling, drawing him away from his dream. The rush of the train is real now, Simon hears it often from his bed, he turns the light on. The fox skull is facing him, he looks at his body, he's inside the sleeping bag. The door to the bedroom creaks, Jane floats in, eyes stuck shut.

"Take the witchth to the church, or they steal mummy," she says.

14

KRAM ARMY

Tuesday, 8 am, 25 degrees.

The sky is blue again, toast pops out of the toaster.
The man on the radio says the harlequin ladybirds
have reached as far north as Humberside, and there
have been sightings near Scarborough. Simon hears
Hull as Hell. Emptying the contents of a box of
Weetabix on the kitchen table, he slips his hand into
the dark. The Dr. Who card he's after sticks under a
nail, he shifts in his chair and sees the reflection of
his mother in the milk at the bottom of his bowl.
Anne puts a large pink pill in her mouth and swallows
it with a glass of water.

"What are they for, mum?" asks Simon.

"Ibuprofen, love, for my knees. Will you do the stairs
for me, please?"

"The ladybirds are coming from Hell," says Simon
flicking at the Dr. Who card.

"Can you help, please, love?"

"I'm going to!" Simon picks up the pan and brush from the utility room, climbs to the top of the stairs and flicks the ladybirds into the pan.

"They're coming through the window," says Anne, sweat beading on her brow.

"Like the locusts past Nottingham," whispers Simon.

"They are good for the roses, love, they eat the greenfly. Don't forget you have swimming tonight." Anne points at the folded towel and black trunks on top of the washing machine.

"I swam for the County," she says, handing him a small booklet with *Swimming for Schoolboys* printed on the front.

Bovril prevents that sinking feeling, reads the advert on the back. Simon tucks it into his haversack and heads for school. Rubba is whistling 'Living Thing' and leaning against the bricks between the cul de sacs.

"I've got something to show you after school," says Rubba, tapping his nose.

Simon has Music first; the class sit quietly on the terrazzo floor. They will be playing the glockenspiel and singing 'The Fisher Boy'. Mrs. Miggins looks painfully slim in a yellow jumper and black dress. She hands out the lyric sheets.

I waited on the beach while around me dashed
        the water,
I waited on the beach, but alas no father came,
Son now I am a stranger exposed to every danger,
Cried the poor little fisher boy so far away
        from home.

Visions of places pass in Simon's head, some real, others made up. Hares, sharks, ghosts, ladybirds, knees of rubber, knees that swell, bending bones and children trapped underground. The thoughts rotate like the slide show projected once a year onto the serving hatch at home.

After school, Rubba and Simon meet by the iron gate and head for the newsagents. The bell over the door rings, the inside of the shop smells of bubble gum dust and fountain pen ink. Rubba pulls Simon over to the racks of magazines and picks out a title.

"Remember the kids in America?" Rubba whispers excitedly.

"Why are you whispering?" Simon takes the magazine, flicks it open to a double page spread of adverts. Skateboards with multicoloured wheels, metal trucks and sparkling grip tape explode across the pages.

"You can buy everything we saw before Jaws, in here."

"How much is the blue one with the red wheels?" asks Simon.

"That's called a Grentec Coyote, twenty-five quid, on mail order," says Rubba.

A voice from behind starts.

"That magazine is 60 pence boys, buy it, or put it back where you found it," croaks the shopkeeper, picking sunburned skin between the freckles on his forehead.

"Go and buy some sweets, Radda," whispers Rubba.

Simon goes to the counter and buys a pack of Cola flavoured Blobs, and a bag of Gold Rush chewing gum with the five pence kept in the bottom of his sock. They exit the newsagents and lean against the red post box in front of Fred's chip shop. Simon opens the Blobs and Rubba pulls the Skateboard magazine from his haversack.

"You stole it!" Simon looks nervously at the door of the shop.

"I just want good things to happen, I wish we had a skateboard, that's all."

"Stealing isn't right,"

"We spend twenty pence a day in there."

"It doesn't make it right."

"We'll hide it at the camp," says Rubba.

"I don't think the camp's safe now, the Seaburn Batlads will get wind, if they haven't already. The trophy we found in the gorse is probably theirs too," says Simon.

"I don't want to get stung with nettles down my pants. We need to think about survival now, I've got four unopened packets of Fruit Pastilles under my bed."

"That won't be enough. Lenny said his trumpet brings up ghosts," says Simon.

"We'll need the kind of army that can handle the living, and the dead," says Rubba.

"But there's only three of us," says Simon.

"I found something in the safe at the back of the garage, something that will stop them, don't worry, the Potts know how to do things, proper," says Rubba, pulling his cocked trigger finger through the air.

15

ARMIES NEED CEMETERIES

Friday, 4 pm, 26 degrees.

"Meet me by the old oak tree," said Simon to Squeaky and Rubba after school. After tea, the boys converge on the corner of the cul-de-sac, and head to the gorse camp next to the oak.

"You know that leveret we caught in the rabbit run over by the train tracks?" says Simon, kicking a stone along the parched soil.

"The day after we ran from the Batlads? Yeah," says Squeaky.

"It died and we buried it, by the tree," says Simon pointing.

"You were supposed to let it go."

"And you were supposed to eat it."

Squeaky whimpers, Rubba sighs.

"It was an accident, you were hungry, it's not your fault," Simon puts his arm around Squeaky.

"We've got to start an army, before the ghosts get out

of the cracks and we get nettles shoved where they shouldn't," hurries Rubba.

"At least my dad buried Tiny near our camp," says Simon.

"Armies need cemeteries to survive. We need to be like the Mice of Tobruk in my comic, small, and dangerous," says Rubba polishing the nails of his right hand on his shirt.

"Who is going to be scared of an army that's named after mice?" Simon's head is cocked.

"Elephants," says Squeaky.

"The Mice of Tobruk went radgie in North Africa in the war, they were living down tunnels and fighting Germans," says Rubba.

"Which war, the first one, or the second?" asks Simon.

"The cool war."

"Which one was cool?"

"All wars are cool, otherwise why have them?" says Rubba, looking at the horizon.

"We've got tunnels," whispers Squeaky.

"And the real stuff," says Rubba, tapping the lump in his pocket.

"Is it that plastic one you brought to school and got sent home for?" says Simon, picking his own stem of long grass and chewing the sweet white tip.

"This one's from the safe at the back of my dad's garage," says Rubba.

"Like the magnifying glass that sets other kid's dad's cars on fire?"

"Better than that, this one's from the barracks at Otterburn."

"Whatever you say, Rubba. Come on, I'll show you where we buried Tiny." Simon leads them to the edge of the roots of the old oak tree. Jane's lollipop cross lies snapped next to a freshly dug hole.

"She's been taken!" shouts Simon.

"This is a job for the Mice of Kramlin," says Rubba, hands on hips, gipping his neck forward like a bird.

"We should be called the Kram Army. There's no elephants round here, unless the circus comes," says Squeaky.

"We should be known for what we really stand for," says Simon, as he slides the corrugated iron at the camp's entrance to the side.

"What do we stand for?" quizzes Rubba

"Playground battles, fishing, and outdoor survival," replies Simon, crawling into the belly of the gorse, the interior opening out, the air still, like the inside of a house.

In the center of the camp Tiny's body is laid out on

top of a yellow box, black flies dance around her dusty body. The letters S and B are scratched crudely into the gorse needles in front of the box. Simon picks her limp body up. With tears welling from behind the wall, he brushes the dust from her fur and gently places her down on the dried ground. He opens the box, and a harlequin ladybird slides from underneath a piece of yellow paper. Shaggy dog stories, never complete, is written in spidery red writing across the paper.

"Is this what war is like?" asks Squeaky, gorse needles falling from his crooked knees.

"Spit on your hand and join yours with mine," says Simon, putting his hand over the dead leveret. Squeaky and Rubba spit and place their hands on top of each other.

"We are The Conker Boys," says Simon.

"I like that name, Radda," says Rubba.

"Conkers, or conquering, it keeps our enemies guessing and earns a bit of respect before anything starts," says Simon.

"I'm hungry," says Squeaky patting his tummy.

"Armies march on their stomachs," says Rubba.

"Listen!" Squeaky cups his ears, the sound is coming closer.

The high-pitched squeal of an engine vibrates. The

boys crawl to the camp's entrance, a teenage girl in bell
bottoms and a Batman T-shirt is riding a white trial bike
through the entrance of the cul de sac, her long black
hair obscures a passenger's face. Accelerating, she lifts
the front wheel to jump the kerb, the back wheel
bounces up, her hair moves to the side and the familiar
face behind her bobs up and down. The bike hugs the
hawthorn hedge leading to Stickleback Forest then turns
sharply, aims for the gorse, blue smoke spewing from its
exhaust.

"Abandon camp!" shouts Simon, and they scurry for
the entrance.

The girl shrieks a blood curdling, "Ahhhhyeeeeyaa."
Swinging the bike she slides the back wheel out in front
of them, soil and debris peppers the gorse bush like
shrapnel. The Conker Boys turn and scramble back into
the camp. The engine splutters, then stops dead.

"Follow me," says Rubba, crawling past Tiny's stiff
body to the back.

"Cornered," comes a mocking voice followed by three
sharp notes of a trumpet. Lenny of the Seaburn Batlads
sneers, chlorophyll teeth flashing through the branches.
Rubba crawls on, calling the Conker Boys to keep up, he
tears a hole in a sheet of polythene at the back, where
the gorse peters out and a dried-out swamp begins.

Simon and Squeaky scramble through the gap in the blue plastic. Lenny and his trumpet follow, the sound of brass pierces the humid air.

"He's playing our song," says Squeaky.

"Where's your mama gone?" spits Simon. A clump of bulrushes point thick brown seedheads into the sky, crusts like cracked plates form a dirty skin of mud over rotting vegetation.

"Woke up this morning and my mama was gone," sings Rubba.

"Pack it in, man," snarls Squeaky.

"Through the bulrushes," whispers Simon and they slide on their bellies atop the mud, the stench of the past creeps through the cracks like nappies left out in the sun. Bulrush stems snap as they clamber. Lenny's at the edge of the swamp, waving blue polythene, a sucking sound coming from where he's stood. Simon sees the entrance to a tunnel running under the spine road, the Conker Boys slide on the slop and reach the culvert. Lenny roars in frustration, the mud wants his shoes, for keeps.

"In the tunnel we go," whispers Simon crouching into the cool blackness. The sound of their own breath and footsteps echo. The circle of light at the entrance dies as they push on into the black unknown.

"When will it be over?" asks Squeaky.

"We'll see the light," says Simon.

Holding each other's T-shirts, they shuffle, a hum rumbling above.

"What's that sound?" asks Rubba.

"Cars on the spine road," says Simon.

"I want to go home," says Squeaky.

"We've got no choice but to keep on going," says Simon.

"Who was the girl on the bike?" asks Rubba.

"Might've been a witch sent by Tiny, Squeaky's grandad knows where all the animal spirits go," mumbles Simon.

"Don't talk like that, Radda," says Squeaky.

"Why?"

"I've seen her before," says Squeaky.

"The leveret or the girl?" asks Simon.

"The girl."

A football sized circle of light appears, growing with their steps until it hurts to look. They climb over a log covered in stickleback skin twisted like silver paper. The sunlight burns the world.

"We found a way into the reservoir!" Rubba raises his fist in triumph at the top of the concrete slope running down to a dwindling pond of dirty water. Dry weed and bleached stones lie scattered across the flat grey surface.

"Soon it'll be just fish bones," says Simon.

"I'm thirsty," says Squeaky.

"We better find another way out,"

16

SWIMMING LESSONS

Squeaky reckons a badger made the run they use to get out under the fence. It's big enough for ten-year-olds and they make their way back to the spine road. A pine martin is dragging a crow by the neck down the central reservation as they cross and join the zig zag path. Simon gets home in time for a swimming lesson, rushing up the stairs to the bathroom to wash the remnants of swamp from his hands with soap from the Avon lady. Anne makes him a sandwich. He collects a towel and trunks from the utility room, mother and son walk the flagstones, through the gate, and climb into the heavy doored Hillman. Sunshine makes surface things feel better, the bus stop by the Bay Horse sparkles, twinkles like it was made of gems, silver and gold. On toward the chimneys of Blyth power station, and the swimming baths down the road.

"I'm going to have to stop, my knee hurts, love," Anne pulls the car into The Delaval Arms.

Anne is wearing red shorts, her left knee bandaged

heavily, two safety pins stick from the bandage, top and bottom.

"Can you go in and get me some water, please, love?" asks Anne, adjusting the bandage.

"Yes, mum, I will."

Simon walks across the car park, the pub perched high on sandstone cliffs, below them, Collywell Bay and a wreck of rocks stolen from land by the power of the sea. The horizon clashes two shades of blue, St. Mary's lighthouse glows like a white tube in the sunshine. A polished rock sits on a pedestal outside the pub, inscribed with the shaft wheel of Hester Pit. Simon reads the first line describing the rescue, the one his teacher wouldn't fully explain at school. His squirrel jumps off the thought and he enters the pub. The beanpole barman in a black shirt runs a tap and gives Simon a glass of water.

"Wish on the stone. If you mean well, it should come true," says the barman.

"Are the people still down there?"

"Don't talk like that, bonny lad."

"I listened, to learn."

"The truth is everywhere and hard to find,"

Simon leaves with the glass of water, stopping to sit on the Bluestone.

'I don't want any more chores,' he whispers to himself and kisses the salty rock. Out to sea, a yellow boat and a black buoy are anchored in front of St. Mary's. In the distance a family of four wade through the rock pool, shoes on their hands, the tide chasing them to higher ground. Simon walks to the car and hands Anne the water through the driver's window.

"There's something in the glass, love."

Simon scoops the insect out and throws it down.

"It bit me." Simon sucks his finger.

"Show me," says Anne, taking his hand into hers.

"You can't see it, mum, but I felt it," says Simon.

"It must've been a ladybird, love. Did you make a wish?" Anne takes a pink tablet from a child proof container and swallows it down with the water.

"For your pain to go away," says Simon, looking at the dead ladybird in the gravel, Adam's apple clicking in his neck.

"Pain is part of life, love, you get on with it, and good people help."

Simon thinks about his wishes, one for himself and one for his mother.

"I need to do more chores, mum."

"I'll give you more when you learn to brush the stairs properly."

Anne turns the key and drives down the sea front to Blyth. The long arm of the south pier reaches into the waves like a broken embrace. Over the river, the power station's two chimneys climb. Distance changes sight, and water washes away time. Anne parks the car in front of the swimming baths. Simon helps her up the steps, she kisses him on the cheek and he heads to the changing rooms. He changes and walks through the shallow water of the verruca bath slowly. Anne waves to him from the café as he enters the main hall. The pool lanes are separated with floating rope. A man is swimming front crawl, a row of rubber bricks lie at the bottom of the deep end, the dark shapes distorting in the overhead light. The swimming instructor leads the lesson, she's tall, with high pointed cheekbones, straight blonde hair, dressed in a black tracksuit, the arms covered in brightly coloured badges. Ten children stand poolside.

"I want you to hold your noses, jump into the water, take your bottoms off, tie a knot in each pantleg, grab the waist tight and blow air into the pyjama bottoms." Mrs. Felton's stern voice bounces off the tiling, on the count of three they jump in.

Simon feels the air rush up his pyjamas, he reaches down to push the bubbles out, the material clinging to his body like polyester skin. The man in the public lane is swimming butterfly, the pyjama children tread water. The ripped yellow Lilo washed on the beach in Jaws arrives in Simon's head, driving his squirrel across the branches and him into a frantic crawl. He reaches the side in panic, raises his belly on to the tiles and skins his shins. A red drop trickles from his shin into the water.

Mrs. Felton stands over him, arms folded tight.

"Get changed, we can't have you bleeding in the pool."

Simon shuffles back through the verruca bath and sits on the long pine bench in the changing room. The man who swam butterfly strides in dripping, head shaved, tattooed tear under his left eye, swallow between thumb and index finger.

"Do you know, Steven?" he asks, drying himself with a long white towel that touches the ground and picks up a stray droplet of Simon's blood.

"Steven?" Simon replies.

"Aye, Squeaky," says the man.

"From school?"

"Watch for him." The man stares, sliding his neck forward.

"I will," says Simon, forgetting the cut on his shin.

17

NAMES ON THE MONUMENT

Thursday, 9 am, 23 degrees.

The pupils ready for New Hartley. Simon joins the queue for the bus. The yellow interior smells of diesel and old smoke. Simon can feel his breakfast arguing with his stomach as the bus pulls up next to the Chinese takeaway. The village of New Hartley looks the same as old Kramlin, but there are no new houses here, yet. The school children file off. Keks grabs Simon by the arm, dragging him out of sight behind the bus and over the road to a news agent.

"Tell the shop keeper your mother's ill and you want a packet of Players No. 7 'cos she can't walk."

"My mum's leg is bad, how did you know?"

"Everyone knows, get the cigs, and quick before the tekka sees."

Simon moves toward the counter. The server wears a bright green jumper, a mop of crow black hair loiters on a crumbly face that looks like old plaster.

"My mum is ill, she wants cigarettes."

"Have you just moved in, son?"

"No, I mean, yes..."

"They're not for your mam, are they kidda?"

"No, she says people who smoke die when they're young."

"Your mam's not wrong there, bonny lad, here, you can have a single for five pence. I'll sell you as many as you want when you look old enough."

"Thanks, mister."

Simon exits the shop and gives Keks the cigarette.

"Where's the packet?"

"He would only give me one and I paid for it, here's your money back."

"Put it behind your ear, Radda," says Keks taking the money into his lumpen hands.

"Why don't you put it behind your ear?" Keks knuckles the top of Simon's arm, leaving him to walk over to the memorial, grimacing.

"Under this ground the miners were trapped with their children," says the teacher. Simon raises his hand.

"What is it now, Radcliffe?"

"Did they get out, sir?"

"Radcliffe."

"Yes, sir?"

"Is that a cigarette behind your ear?"

"Yes, but."

"No buts! Get on the bus, you yellow fingered imbecile!"

The heat has encouraged confectionary dust and sweat to the surface of the seats. The cab is hotching, ungodly. Simon watches the class through the grease-smeared window as they gather round a plinth carved with local names. Keks comes to the bus window and points to his ear. Simon shakes his head and points at the teacher. Keks punches the window, the driver startles from his heat nap. The visit ends and the class file back on the bus. The teacher finishes a hissy head count, sits down next to the driver and lights the confiscated cigarette. Simon looks at the names on the monument as the bus pulls away and throws up into his haversack.

Back at school Simon is called to reception. He practices shaping his palms in preparation for a caning. Auntie June is waiting by the metal filing cabinet near the door, she's wearing a bright red knitted cardigan and a black skirt.

"You're coming home, Simon, love."

They hurry down the cycle path in silence, the door to the utility room is open, a pan of potatoes is half mashed on the kitchen table, the gas burns on an empty stove. Auntie June rests her hand on the three-legged stool and faces Simon.

"Your mum's in hospital, love."

Jane floats to the bottom of the stairs in her nightie. She nods at Simon, points at the calendar on the anaglypta wall and closes her eyes slowly.

18

BOGIES BOARDS & PAIN

Saturday, 11 am, 26 degrees.

Anne took a lot of pain killers and they made a hole in her stomach. Simon heard Auntie June say she could die. Simon stopped those words from meaning anything by taking them and pressing them against the wall. Words are just noises after all, like his name, two syllables stuck together, searching for a meaning. Auntie June puts the kettle on, the water comes to a boil, Simon wasn't watching it, he's thinking about the chores he should have done. Little things seem big when you're small, and that was the God from school's fault. The God of Legs knows what's right and what's wrong on the inside, because Simon made him for himself. Simon looks up the hallway stairs, the steps are littered with yellow and black ladybirds. Jane's put some in a glass jar and placed it at the bottom of the stairs where the calendar fell. Simon tells her to empty them in the back garden. Jane nods, floats through the utility room, onto the soil of the vegetable patch and tips the jar. The insects tumble like heavy black rain. The milky sound of the doorbell bounces around the hallway. Simon sees two figures through the distorted glass, he twists the aluminium of the front door's handle. Squeaky and Rubba are stood at the step, dressed in shorts and matching Montreal Olympics T-shirts.

"We want to make a skateboard with your dad," says Rubba.

"He knows how to make things," says Squeaky.

Simon leads them to the kitchen, past the stool his mother peels carrots on, through the utility room, down the side fence to the garage. Through the orange door Peter is painting bitumen on the chassis of the Hillman. 'Always prepare for the worst, son, then you can say you did your best before things happen,' Peter had told Simon that last winter. Simon's fingers had felt like they would drop off in the cold and the torch batteries were running low. Now, the radio is playing 'No Charge' By J.J Barrie. Squeaky stands over Peter, like a hawk watching for field mice on the spine road.

"Where's your mam?" asks Squeaky.

"In the hospital," Peter replies.

"Are you hungry now?" Simon asks Squeaky.

"I'm always hungry."

"I'll make some sarnies."

Simon goes back into the kitchen and cuts doorstep slices from a loaf of white bread. He smears margarine and dollops of golden honey on the slices then cuts them in half. He looks at the cooker, the pan with the mash potato, still on the hob, he scrapes the mash into the bin and pours warm water into the pan. He's not done that chore before, just seen his mother do it, time and time again. On the way back he looks at the container of pink pain killers and his mother's voice arrives to dance with the squirrel in his head. Anne's telling them about swimming, how to time your breath. Down in the vegetable garden the ladybirds lay like the stray pieces of a boardgame. Simon knows Jane feels things that he can't see. He trips on the step and the sandwiches jolt on the tray. When the squirrel jumps too many branches, things can go sideways.

"We want to make a skateboard, like the ones we saw at the cinema on Squeaky's birthday," says Rubba.

"I see, and how long do you want it?" says Peter.

"Forever," says Rubba.

"That is a long time. I've got some floorboards from a flat in Jesmond at the back of the garage, I'll shape one up and the three of you can sand it down."

Peter hands out scraps of grey coloured sandpaper

and lifts an old floorboard from behind the workbench. Squeaky's eyes follow Peter as he hammers out unwanted nails. Peter moves to the bare brick wall, takes a hanging saw, sketching a nose and tail on the wood with a black and yellow pencil and saws the edges off.

"Gentlemen, over to the sanding team," Peter hands the board to Simon, who lays it out on the paving stones in front of the garage wall. The boys get to work, Squeaky gets a splinter in his thumb. Simon removes it with a pair of tweezers and his mother's voice comes to him: 'That's how to get things done, love.'

'New York Mining Disaster,' by The Bee Gees plays on the radio. Old songs come back on Sundays and Peter tells his stories, where he was, what he was doing, when the songs were first on.

'Have you seen my wife, Mr. Jones,' sing The Bee Gees. Simon waits for Peter to roll out from under the car, but he doesn't come. Simon kneels to look, Peter must have been sweating, two wet spots have appeared next to his face on the concrete. The temperature in the garage drops. Simon looks at a crack in the floor, and two ants crawl out.

Peter hands the boys three small brushes and a tin of varnish. They take the shaped wood into the sunlight, place it on bricks and paint the varnish on to the surface. Soon it has a uniform shine, after the first coat they eat their honey sandwiches and play marbles along the edge of the paving. The varnish dries, Simon notices the ants are stuck in the varnish now, trapped like they were in amber.

"What are you going to do about the wheels?" asks Peter.

Jane has been making a cemetery for the ladybirds in the vegetable patch, she walks over the grass to the shed tucked by the back window of the lounge. The door creaks on entry and she reappears holding a red roller-skate. She skips across the dead grass and hands it to Peter.

"Are you sure?" he asks, hand on her shoulder.

She nods. Peter takes no time stripping the trucks and wheels from the boot and placing them at either end of the board. He marks the holes and drills them like he did Big Boy. The homemade skateboard is ready.

"He's a wizard, your dad," says Squeaky.

"Come on, let's give it a test ride," says Simon.

Simon, Rubba and Squeaky carry the board down the zig zag path to the spine road.

"Nobody has made me anything, before," says Squeaky.

"Some people say your dad is in prison," says Rubba,

kicking cuckoo spit from the long grass. A grasshopper's chirp fills the silence. A swarm of greenfly hovers over the badger run as they squeeze under the gap in the reservoir fence. Simon pushes the board over the top, joins Rubba and Squeaky on the other side. Out on the concrete the reservoir is no more than a big puddle. Simon places the board down.

"It's like the swimming pool in the skateboard film," says Squeaky, jumping on and pushing off. The wood scrapes the ground, swings downhill. The roller skate wheels rattle, Squeaky flails for balance. A wheel catches a stone, the board stops. Squeaky's muted scream is delayed, like he's been fired from a cannon. The board rolls on as Squeaky flies, Simon and Rubba run but it disappears into the murk along with Squeaky.

"I'm drowning!" Squeaky thrashes the surface.

"Stand up man, the rezzy's not deep anymore," shouts Rubba.

Squeaky stands and brown water pours from the pockets of his shorts. They laugh, then remember the skateboard.

"We'll never get it back," says Rubba.

Squeaky climbs out of the dirty water, sits down on the hot ground and takes his socks and shoes off.

Simon strips to his underpants, runs and shallow

dives in. Dirty water rushes past his ears, the voice from the sleeping bag whispers, 'I'm not your sister.'

Simon's lungs begin to burn, something cold brushes his foot. He swims for the sun, straining every muscle. A single magpie swoops across the empty reservoir as Simon breaks the surface.

"It's too far in." He spits the weed from his mouth.

"I didn't even have a go," says Rubba.

"Lenny was right, there are things down there," Simon says, pointing at the dirty water.

"Lenny's just a radgie, and radgies make things up to scare people," says Rubba.

"We can't tell anyone about how we got into the rezzy, if we do, it won't be safe, the Batlads'll come here too," says Squeaky.

"A proper skateboard would work lush here, man, now that all the water has gone," says Rubba.

"We need to make a skateboard with bigger wheels, so they don't catch on stones," Simon pulls weed from his chin and throws it onto the baking concrete.

"Pram wheels are big," says Squeaky.

"I saw a pram at the bottom of the slag heap last week," says Rubba.

"Lenny said that's where the ghosts come up when he plays his trumpet," says Squeaky.

"Ghosts probably only come out when it's dark," says Simon.

The air is wet like the inside of an airing cupboard as the boys walk home, the cracks in the ground are wider than they've ever been. They reach the zig zag path, say their goodbyes, and split.

19

WORDS IN THE HEAD, SICKNESS
IN THE MIDDLE

"Your mum is back from hospital, son," says Peter from
the orange garage door.

"Is she better?"

"They stitched her tummy up like they fixed your
sister's tongue."

"Don't remind me of the bad things I've done."

"She'll be happy to see you, son."

Simon walks toward the back door of the house. He
sees his mum down low through the frosted glass of the
door, he opens it and sees Anne is in a wheelchair.

'I told you it would be too late,' says the sleeping bag
voice.

"It's to stop my knee swelling, love," says Anne.

Simon's sickness slides its fingers up over the wall.

"It's okay, love, good people will help."

"I'll do more chores, mum, I promise."

The wheelchair has two black wheels up front and

two large white wheels with spokes at the back. A strip of black webbed material connects the middle, tightening into a seat when the grey frame is pulled apart and the chair opens.

"Did you miss me?" Anne asks Simon.

"Yes, mum." Simon kisses Anne on the cheek and heads up to his bedroom. The stairs look dusty, Jane is sitting on his bed.

"I'm not the girl in there," she says, pointing at the bottom of the chest of drawers, where he keeps his sleeping bag.

"Brenda is nextht," she says, rubbing the crust from her eyes.

"Next for what?"

"The witches."

"My head is full of the words of someone I've not met and my body feels sick, where my heart is on the inside."

"If you mean well, the spirits will leave you be, sometimes they will help."

"And what if I mean bad?"

"Water changes things, Simon, like daddy knows."

The next day at school Simon tells Squeaky they have to find Tiny and bury her in the grounds of the church. Squeaky asks why and Simon tells him his sister said the spirits will take his mum away if he doesn't. Squeaky says he would never go into a graveyard. Simon decides it's probably not a good idea for him to bury a leveret in a graveyard because the God from school would get confused.

THE SLAG HEAP

Sunday, 10 am, 27 degrees.

Rubba is flicking through the pages of Skateboard magazine in the gorse camp.

"We're never going to have enough money for that Grentec Coyote," says Squeaky.

"Those red wheels look like rubies when the light shines through them," says Rubba.

"We could always go back to selling rose petals and bulrushes round the doors like last Summer, keep on going until we have enough money for a skateboard. My mum will write a cheque and send it off to the magazine for us. When it comes, we can share it, a Grentec Coyote will belong to everyone in The Conker Boys," says Simon.

"Penny for the guy comes after summer, when Squeaky plays dead in a wheelbarrow, we always make good money," says Rubba.

"Your dad could make another skateboard with bigger

wheels, and we could pull Squeaky round, with jam on his lips for blood," says Simon.

"Blood always makes good money," says Rubba.

"We need to get the pram wheels from the slag heap before someone else gets them, useful things don't stay out for long," says Simon.

"The big cardboard boxes round the back of Presto get taken fast too," says Squeaky.

"Let's get some stuff to eat and drink from Radda's and head out for the pram wheels, before someone else gets them," says Rubba.

In the Radcliffe utility room, Squeaky and Rubba play with the front wheels of Anne's wheelchair. Simon grabs a packet of Bourbon biscuits and fills a used Robinson's bottle with water, squeezes in Jif lemon and adds a pinch of sugar from the bowl by the kettle.

"Leave my mum's wheelchair alone," says Simon as Rubba spins one of the back wheels.

"Are things bad at home?" asks Squeaky.

"He put his mam in there," says Rubba.

"It was the spirits," spits Simon.

"We need to go to mine," says Rubba.

"Why?" asks Simon

"Protection," answers Rubba.

"The Conker Boys should fight clean."

"But we're the Kram Army."

"We settled on The Conker Boys, and you spat on it, so it stays that way," says Simon.

They walk the cycle track on their way to Rubba's.

"That girl Becky lives down there."

"Do you think her hair has grown back?"

"Not much, it takes ages for hair to grow long."

"Do you think she found the trophy?"

"It's probably the one we found in our camp."

"Is it our camp? And our camp only?"

"What do you mean?"

"Tiny got dug up, that upset the spirits twice over. A dead leveret is a mistake but grave robbing is the work of devils, and don't forget that message about the shaggy dog stories," says Simon.

"We are inside a shaggy dog story now," says Squeaky.

"And none of us has a dog," says Rubba.

"You've got a ferret."

"It's not mine, it's my dad's, he uses it for ratting."

They arrive at Rubba's house, he unlocks the door, the house is empty. They walk through the hallway and kitchen to the back garden. Rubba leads them past a cage where a white ferret is sleeping, the garage door is unlocked. The inside of the garage is dark, the strip light flickers on, a blue plastic sheet is pulled over a motorbike. A helmet with red insignia hangs on the wall above a grey uniform. Next to the bike is a black safe, Rubba kneels and takes something plum green, round and the size of a tennis ball from it. Rubba slips it into a brown leather satchel he picks from the wall.

"Come on we need to get the pram wheels before some radgies get to them first," says Simon.

"What have you got?" asks Squeaky, pointing at the satchel, Rubba winks the way grown-ups do when it just feels wrong.

They walk past the chip shop and head down the cycle path toward the slag heap.

"Is it true your mam is in a wheelchair because of you? Brassa said his mam knows someone on your street and that's what she told him, " asks Rubba.

"It's because he doesn't do his chores," Squeaky answers.

"At least my mum doesn't drink Babycham," says Simon, regretting it as it's coming out of his gob.

Squeaky's face distorts.

"I'm sorry, Squeaky. It was a witch that made my mum ill," says Simon.

"A witch?"

"Hares turn into witches when they want. Tiny was a baby hare, she was working with the girl, the one that talks with the squirrel in my head," says Simon.

"You've inhaled varnish, Radda," says Rubba.

"The last time it rained I was in my sleeping bag, and a girl spoke to me."

"It was probably just your sister, hiding in a cupboard."

"It wasn't my sister but she does know what's happening, she's connected to it."

"Connected to what?"

"The cracks in the ground."

"Did you tell anyone about the voice in your head?" asks Rubba.

"People would say that it wasn't happening."

"Then they would send you to the school nurse and they would steal you from your parents," says Squeaky folding his arms.

"I've been trying to work out what the voice is telling me."

"What is it then?"

"I thought it might be coming from the face on the clay pipe in my sock drawer. I found it in the farmers field when it was last ploughed. Lenny said that the ghosts were coming out through the ground, didn't he?"

"How many people are down there?" asks Squeaky.

"Everyone gets buried, in the end," Simon taps his foot and a ladybird crawls over the coal dust, shining in the material of his sand shoe.

"Some people go early," says Rubba, thumbing his satchel.

"People who go early want to be heard," says Simon.

"Who went early?" asks Squeaky.

"Those names," says Simon.

"Which names?"

"Your name was on that monument at New Hartley," says Simon.

"But Sam derailed the Flying Scotsman train," whispers Squeaky.

"For a reason, Squeaky, rich people didn't want the poor people to be heard," says Simon.

The slag heap rises like an industrial pimple on the face of the New Town. The Cheviots are looking fake again but it's the pile of rock in the middle of the estate that was made by man. Mr. Tebbins said it was like that because there was nowhere else for the rock to go. Peter said life was cheap, who is stopping it from being cheap right now? Simon asks the God of Legs for an answer but he's not talking to the squirrel jumping branch to branch, instead he gets a vision, a memory in his head. Last Winter, he'd pulled Jane to the slag heap on a sled. Three feet of snow had fallen over night. Kids woke in a frenzy. The slag heap was all white, like a pyramid covered in ants, tiny black specks hurtled down on sleds and bin bags. When the snow melted, chunks of coal sparkled like diamonds in the winter light. The drone of a bumble bee jumps Simon back into the now.

The boys find the pram upside down in a ditch at the end of the cycle track. Four white rubber wheels pointed up in the long grass.

"We got here in time," says Rubba.

"Let's take it up to the top," says Simon.

They push the pram up the steep slag heap, the burgundy rooves of the estate fan out like the seats in the cinema. The slow green grip of the empty lands hugs tight at the brick border. Over east, the darkness of the sea is interrupted by the chimneys of Blyth power station.

Reaching the top, Simon thinks that only real kings would know this feeling, what it was like to stand at the top of a slag heap with a pram. The Conker boys have taken the highest point of the New Town, the birds are singing hard, and a new skateboard awaits its making in Peter's capable hands. Squeaky climbs in, Radda stands on the front axle facing backwards and Simon clings onto the handle. Radda slides his leather bag to the front, the bulge shining in the sun. One push and the uneven surface shakes them like a trolley riding gravel.

The sound of a high-pitched engine starts to whisper

then rises large, metal wasps are swarming, bombing like they do round the school bin. The noise is coming from multiple angles, an engine screams behind, two bikes flank them, like Border Collies herding sheep, on the grind. Lenny and the black-haired girl are on one scrambler, flame haired Chig and Arma, ride the other two. The Batlads hunt loose and wild. Seeking revenge for dropped nettles, neck punching, screaming Geordie yee haas with evil pride.

The pram hits a dip, the front catches like Jane's box on the stairs, bouncing a somersault, spilling them out like dropped shopping in the Presto precinct. The bikes overshoot, turning round they arc and come once more. Simon sees a drainage tunnel at the end of the cycle path and bellows for The Conker Boys to follow, they hurdle over nettles, sprinting for the black hole they burst in, darkness swallows them whole. Hearts rattle ribs, the boys breathing is out of control. The bikes are coming in, chasing them into the tunnel, orcas driving seals off the ice. A cacophony of sound vibrates, Simon feels his guts shake, Lenny's trumpet the hot icing on the terror cake, pounding tangy metal on the concrete curves. The Conker Boys pass a bend, the bikes' engines rage as the light fades to blue black ink. Simon fumbles against the wall, feels it disappear, there's a space set back. Holding hands, they move into the recess and stand panting. The scream of the engines and Lenny's trumpet closes in, tearing chunks from inside their heads.

"Give it to them, Lenny, underground style," shouts one of the twins.

"He's going to bring them up," hisses Rubba.

"It's ghost time!" shouts Lenny.

The noise stops, scuffling footsteps echo.

"Catch your breath, keep quiet," whispers Simon, hearing the squeak of leather straps, the dark swallows time, dragging it into slow motion.

"Please don't pull the pin," whispers Simon.

A dull click sounds at chest height, a metallic clinking dances from the concrete floor. Polyester rustles, a waft of air brushes Simon's hand, a sharp sound rattles toward the entrance. Lenny's trumpet sounds like the Inter-City's horn passing in the night, then it stops and the metallic rattle continues.

You'll never forget the seconds before something big happens in your life, afterwards it pre-loads in your head more times than you would like, as if your dreams bought a franchise you can't give back. Simon feels his face distorting, cheeks pressing against his teeth, the surface of his eyes burning. The bright yellow flash lasts a second, hot dust and chemical stench floods the tunnel. Rushed footsteps follow a desperate scream, then a thud.

"Squeaky!" Simon shouts, as a pair of arms wrap round his legs.

"Radda," says a voice weakly. Simon bends down to feel the owner of the arms, he feels a hot head, all sticky.

"Rubba. Where's Squeaky?"

"I'm hit."

"Why did you pull the pin if you knew it was real, Rubba?"

"I didn't think it was a real hand grenade, Radda."

"Made up things can hurt too."

"Where's Squeaky?"

"We need to get out and get help."

Rubba holds Simon's hand, and they shuffle toward the entrance. Past the bend, the circle of light shines on the jagged edge of the three-foot hole blown in the tunnel floor. He shouts for Squeaky, his voice echoes in reply. Rubba whimpers, Simon turns, through the smokey light he sees Rubba's face, raw, wet mince.

"We're going to jump, I'll go first, then turn and catch you," says Simon.

Simon dives over the hole toward the tunnel entrance, the smoke ripping strips off his throat. On the other side Lenny's trumpet lays twisted on the floor, broken.

"I'm ready," Rubba jumps, and Simon pulls him over by the arms. Simon kicks the broken trumpet and shouts for Squeaky again. Rubba needs help, at the entrance the world is calm, sometimes things on the inside are scary and from the outside, nothing looks wrong. Above the shell-shocked pair, the shadow of the slag heap looms. What looks like a black beetle is protruding from the side of Rubba's head. Simon heads for the red phone box near the houses across from the cycle track.

"It's 999 for an ambulance, right?"

"Ring my dad, I just want to go home, Radda."

"I haven't got any money for the phone box."

"Please," Rubba points a crooked arm at an old Northumbrian house overlooking the slag heap from the spine road. They walk over, Rubba moans along.

Simon approaches the front of the house, 1862 is carved into the sandstone block above the door. Rubba stands in the rose beds, looking like a zombie and Simon knocks on the door. A rotund man in a red golfing jumper appears, face stern, agitated.

"Good lord, what on God's earth is going on?"

"There's been an explosion in the tunnel, and someone's still stuck inside."

"Did you not think to use the phone box, boy?"

"We haven't got any money."

"It costs nothing to call 999, but you wouldn't know that, you look like you don't listen, like the rest of the rats round here."

Rubba stumbles and collapses on a rose bush, cutting his fingers on the thorns.

"The state of him! Clean boy, come inside. Blood boy, stay on the step, if you can make it that far."

"Thanks, mister," says Simon.

"Do I know you?"

Simon sees the golf clubs in the hallway, a red towel hanging from the bag, a Brentford Nylons logo stitched into it.

THE CANE TOAD

Monday, 8 am, 26 degrees.

Pristine New Town homes cast long shadows in the morning sun. Anne is making corned beef sandwiches, Rice Krispies crackle in Simon's bowl. The man on the radio is talking about frying eggs on the pavement, way down the train tracks in London town.

"When is this heat going to give over?" Anne says, looking through the window from her wheelchair.

"I think more ladybirds are going to come."

"You don't seem yourself, love, what's wrong?"

"The cracks in the ground are getting bigger and bigger, baked open by the sun."

Simon squeezes out from behind the kitchen table, opens the fridge door and slips an egg into his pocket.

"Your packed lunch is in the Tupperware, love," says Anne.

"Thanks, mum." Simon heads out of the utility room, over the concrete slabs, white fascia boards glaring, the silica in the road sparkles. There's a gap in the concrete by the caravan, ants with wings are crawling out. Simon didn't sleep well last night; he's been thinking about Squeaky. If he tells people what happened he could lose both of his close friends. Rubba's older brother was in Borstal and Simon thinks Rubba will go to kid jail if he tells adults about the fake hand grenade that happened to be real. Because made up things hurt too. Maybe Squeaky is dead, his mum had him halfway there with rickets and Babycham. Fear breaks the branches the squirrel climbs on, and scary thoughts have stopped him from talking. Even though he knows that its wrong.

Rubba is whistling 'Muskrat Love' in the cut between the cul de sacs, the side of his head has been shaved into a half Mohican. A raised slice across his scalp has a row of black stitches through it, as if a ragworm has been stuck to his temple.

"Your head's amazing, I've always wanted a cool scar," says Simon.

"Did they find Squeaky?"

"The council probably tried to visit his mum, I bet Joe was out poaching in Presto when they came."

"Joe's keep net is still in the gorse camp," says Rubba.

"If Squeaky isn't at school, we should use it to get

down into the hole. We could send your dad's ferret into the tunnel to sniff Squeaky out," says Simon.

At school they call out 'here' in registration and shuffle into assembly. The headmaster strides in with an inappropriate smile. An older man with a bald head and round belly follows behind.

"The honorable Joe Gormley from The National Union of Mineworkers is here to speak to us today. Mr. Gormley opened the remembrance garden in New Hartley, some of you visited it this week," says the headmaster.

Joe Gormley steps forward to the sound of coughs and whispering.

"Clap, children, clap!" shouts the headmaster. A halfhearted ripple rises and falls.

Mr. Gormley is dressed in a gravy brown suit, a custard yellow shirt, bald head with a few strands swept like shredded nylon over a boiled egg. He nods toward the fidgeting wall of boredom and starts reading a poem from a slim green book.

"The Hartley men are noble, and
Ye'll hear a tale of woe;
I'll tell the doom of the Hartley men —
The year of sixty two."

The assembly stands, faces stony, the poem has too many words and some of them sound like the person who wrote the poem, invented them. The President of The National Union of Mineworkers has a face like dried marzipan clinging to stale cake. Someone at the back laughs, and the piano starts. They start to sing Abide with Me, Keks leans into a shaft of light, blowing bubbles of spit from his mouth.

Simon pulls the egg from his pocket, cups it in his palm.

"Why?" mouths Rubba.

"Meet me on the tarmac behind the tuck shop at break," whispers Simon.

Simon heads to his Home Economics class. All the windows are pinned wide, hot air blows in from the outside, break time comes and the corridors seethe with children, jostling for a place on the sticky tarmac. Simon jumps a game of marbles by the drain, runs behind the tuck shop at the side of the playground and pulls the egg out.

"Throw it at him!" shouts Rubba, pointing at Keks, who has stolen midget gems spilling from his mouth.

"Squeaky loved boiled eggs," says Simon looking wistfully over the school roof at the slag heap, wondering if his friend is still breathing. He shakes his head, breaks the egg, it slides out of its shell and slips out on to the playground.

"You wazzock," laughs Rubba.

"Watch," says Simon, willing it to cook on the hot tarmac like the egg cracked on the pavement in London. It slithers into the heat crippled grass and Mrs. Shields, the dinner lady, arrives, hands on hips, face quivering.

"You two, Headmaster's office, now!"

Simon and Rubba traipse across the playground, through the double doors that lead to the headmaster's office. Mrs. Shields follows and knocks on the headmaster's door. She lets herself in, the boys listen at the door, jumping back when she reappears with the headmaster.

"Where's the one with the funny legs," says Mr. McAdam.

"He's under a tunnel, sir, and no one cares about it, apart from us."

"Be quiet!"

"Yes, sir," they reply.

"Why were you defacing the school playground?"

"We were trying to fry an egg, sir," says Simon.

"Not getting enough food to feed your freckly face?" The headmaster's monstrous head looks misplaced on his narrow shoulders.

"A man fried an egg on the pavement in London yesterday," mumbles Simon, chin to chest, eyes staring at his sunburned knees.

"Don't believe everything you read, that's if you can read, the New Town is stuffed with cling ons, like you two," growls the headmaster.

"It was on the radio," says Simon.

"Stand here, palms up," says the headmaster, pointing at the edge of his desk.

The boys shuffle to the designated point of pain, hands out, as if bearing invisible gifts. Mr. McAdam produces a thin cane from a drawer and stands sideways at the front of the desk, barrel chest huffed full of rotting opinions. Simon watches his reflection in the headmaster's glasses as the cane whips down like a bamboo guillotine. Gritting his teeth, the thin strip rips into his soft hands.

"Steven Squire is trapped underground, sir," says Simon quietly.

"No one asked you to speak, boy, next!"

Rubba steps up and offers his palms, the cane swishes. He holds the pain in, to win a little back from the situation.

"Anymore vandalism and you will be expelled. Do you understand?"

"Yes sir," they say in unison.

"Now, get out of my sight," orders the headmaster, a tickle of spittle landing on Simon's cheek.

After school Rubba and Simon compare the welts on their palms as they walk to the gorse camp.

"No one is looking out for Squeaky," says Simon.

"His dads probably got him," says Rubba.

"He hasn't got a dad." Simon catches Rubba's eye.

"Do you believe that? Everyone's got a dad, otherwise, you wouldn't get made, it's the storks and bumble bees' stuff." Rubba tries to push a stone on top of a flying ant with his shoe.

"Some dads die," says Simon.

"And some disappear, leave home," says Rubba.

"You shouldn't leave children when they're not big enough," says Simon.

"You are supposed to stay and make them big on the inside," agrees Rubba, making sure the ant is dead.

"Even if you don't like them," says Simon.

"Especially if you don't like them," agrees Rubba.

"We could use the keep net to lower your dad's ferret into the hole in the tunnel," says Simon.

"And then what?"

"If we get the ferret to sniff my half of Big Boy, then if Squeaky has his, it'll smell it. We've got to try something, or it's between us and the Seaburn Batlads to take the blame for it."

"If he's not dead already, he will die."

"He's not going to die, Rubba, The Conker Boys stick things back together when they fall apart."

21

HADAWAY & WHITE

Simon pulls the keep net open and threads a piece of rope through the top hoop of the opening. A shadow in the shape of a man appears at the entrance to the gorse, the boys fear it's another Batlad attack. A tall man dressed in jeans and a black T-shirt with a red Esso logo in the middle, stands on the skid marks left by the motorbike at the entrance to the camp. Head shaved, his gold earring gleams in one of his jug ears, forehead square like a Kramlin house brick.

"Were you boys with Steven?"

"Squeaky is in the tunnel, mister," says Rubba.

"A boy blew a hole in it with a hand grenade, we were being chased by a gang by the slag heap. I told the head tekka, but nobody listens at school," says Simon.

"They call the big lad Lenny?" says the man looking at the net. Simon nods.

"There was a girl too, Radda reckons she's a witch," says Rubba.

"They call me Billy, I'll write an address down on this

paper, the place is over in Kitty Brewster, red door, number eleven, if you hear anything about Steven, come and let me know." Billy taps the paper with his index finger, takes a note pad and pen from his back pocket and starts to write. Simon sees the swallow tattoo on Billy's hand. The smell of chlorine floats a memory past the squirrel in his brain.

"Make sure you come to Kitty Brewster if you hear anything, anything at all. You know what families are like,"

"Yes, mister."

Billy leaves and Simon and Rubba go back to Simon's house to get his half of Big Boy. They knock the wheelchair over in the utility room, it clatters against the fridge freezer, Anne calls, the boys keep quiet, creep up the stairs. Simon slides open his sock drawer and Rubba marvels at the contents.

"Can I have that bent bullet," whispers Rubba.

"What do you want to swap it for?"

"My dad's ferret, we can get it when he's out, make it look like it escaped."

"I would only want to borrow your dad's ferret, otherwise your dad would find out and come up here looking for it." Rubba looks glum, Simon sighs and gives him the bent bullet.

"Since your dad was in the army, at least it's going to a good home."

Anne limps into the room with the aid of her aluminium walking stick.

"Oh, boys, I thought I heard something, you scared me. Can you help me to the bed, Simon?" Anne sits on Simon's bed and places both her hands on her swollen knee. The sleeping bag is sticking out from under the bed.

"You'll not need that in this heat, love."

"I play inside it when it rains."

"Well, your dad picked it up in Nelson Village from a pitman on a Roundtable charity drive, we should have really passed it on. Dad has done a lot for folk round here over the years, heart of a lion, your dad."

"We're going out, mum, I might be back late."

"Okay, love, have fun."

Simon taps at his half of Big Boy in his pocket and they head over to Rubba's house. When they arrive, Rubba's dad is visible through the lounge window, he's dressed in a green uniform and practicing a salute in the mirror. They wait outside in the bushes, Rubba's dad leaves the house and marches off to the social club holding on tight to his military stories. Inside the house, the boys move through the hallway, to the kitchen that opens straight into the back garden. The path is covered in burns, where Rubba sets paper cap ammo off with a stone. The boys stop at the chicken wire cage that houses the ferret. Rubba opens the side door and lifts the wiry creature out, it's face like a beefed-up psycho rat, body long and thin as Rubba's arm. The ferret's fur is almost white, two pink eyes stare like cake decorations guiding pin prick teeth toward anything worth biting.

"Does it do what you say?" asks Simon.

"My dad says you can't control ferrets, they control you, it's called Hadaway, not that a name makes any difference in how he carries on."

'Leave it to me,' comes the voice from the sleeping bag in Simon's head, the first time Simon's heard it in the presence of another person.

"You looked different then," says Rubba, scrunching his face.

"I was thinking about getting Squeaky out of the hole in the tunnel. If the ferret can lock on to the smell of Big Boy, it could lead us to Squeaky."

Simon holds his piece of conker out and Rubba lifts the ferret to the yellow chestnut core. Hadaway thrashes in his grip, wrapping around Rubba's wrist then running up his arm, scrambling for his neck and sinking its teeth into Rubba's Adam's apple.

"Hadaway, man," squeals Rubba.

The ferret hangs from the punctured skin, body frozen.

'Drop,' comes the voice in Simon's head and Hadaway lets go of Rubba's skin, tumbling to the ground. The ferret stands on its back legs, pink eyes fixed on the half conker in Simon's hand.

'Ready,' comes the voice from the sleeping bag.

"He's trained on the smell of Big Boy, come on, let's go and get Squeaky out the tunnel."

"I can't Radda, I've got to have my tea now."

"I won't tell anyone about the hand grenade. I'll say it was the same thing that happened under the monument at New Hartley."

"What happened at New Hartley?"

"People were trying to come out from the cracks in the ground, the ones who no one listens to."

"I have to have my tea, Radda, I'm starving."

"Squeaky was hungry before this started Rubba. He's got one half of Big Boy and we said we'd never let the pieces be apart,"

23

OPERATION SQUEAKY

Simon empties his school haversack on his bed. He'll need his dad's diving torch, the tokens from the Casper the Friendly Ghost board game, his half of Big Boy, some Robinsons Barley Water, a handful of Bourbon biscuits, a bike pump, and the rubber inner tube from under the family caravan. He cuts some bread and makes a doorstep sandwich with honey, wrapping it in the middle pages of The Evening Chronicle. Anne and Peter are out taking Jane to her first swimming lesson. Simon is on his own, left with instructions for the rotary phone. It's 999 for an ambulance and you must remember your address so they come to the right home.

He puts on his black pants with the extra pockets and slides on some winter socks. He unscrews the studs from his ankle-high rugby boots and puts them on. He puts on his green T-shirt and shrugs into his fish tail parker, handed down. He pulls out the fur the leveret shed in his pocket, removes the sweet wrappers, and biscuit crumbs. Adds a packet of Chewits from the medicine drawer, picks up his penknife and a peeled golf ball, opens the chest freezer and pulls two fish fingers from the Birdseye box. He exits the utility room door and walks across the paving stones. The ladybirds Jane collected from the stairs have been eaten by something. The cul de sac is empty. He pulls the gate shut, slides under the caravan, pulls out the rubber inner tube. Looping it over his right shoulder he heads out over the dead grass to the gorse camp. He kicks at the marks left by the motorbike, slides the corrugated iron across the entrance by the old oak tree. Scurrying into the center of the camp he picks up the keep net. Rubba could be ready for a Borstal tear, Squeaky for a wooden box, the memory of the sound of the hand grenade replays in his head, clicking like a record stuck on the stereo. He exits the camp with the keep net, skirts the zig zag path, finds the cycle track to Rubba's house. Hiding in the bushes, he flicks a stone at the front bedroom window. The orange curtains move, Rubba comes to the window and cracks it open.

"It's time to get Hadaway," hurries Simon.

"Shh, me dad's in," says Rubba, his face poking through the curtains.

"Drop the ferret down in a bag."

Rubba disappears for a few minutes and comes back

with a Presto bag, the end of a ball of wool tied to the handle. Hadaway lies still inside. Rubba lowers him and Simon puts the ferret in the bag inside the green webbing of the keep net.

"Are you sure you're not coming?"

"I can smell my mam's chips frying, Radda. It's mince, mashed snannies and chips tonight."

"Chuck the ball of wool down, I might need it."

"But me mam is making a jumper for me brother to wear in Borstal."

"Does everyone in your family go to Borstal?"

"I haven't been yet."

"Do you want a jumper or Squeaky back from the hole you made with the hand grenade?"

Rubba huffs as Simon catches the ball of wool and waves at the empty window. The smell of chips has made Simon hungry too but he won't touch his bait yet, the ferret comes first. He takes a fish finger and drops it into the Presto bag, Hadaway wriggles, pin teeth bite on defrosting fish. Over the smooth surface of the cycle track Simon trudges. The slag heap grows, until he's where the motorbikes attacked when they somersaulted the pram. He approaches the tunnel behind the ditch, the nettles taller, hungry for skin. He pats the Presto bag and Hadaway's teeth pierce through, catching a finger.

He washes the blood away with barley water and takes a swig.

Entering the tunnel with a deep breath, the sound of water trickles into the darkness. He gets down on all fours at the edge of the hole, he turns the diving torch on, and charges up the Casper the Friendly Ghost pieces. He opens out the keep net and tears the Presto bag open. Hadaway darts into the keep net. Simon attaches the end of the golf ball elastic and a glowing token to the ferret's collar.

He aims the torch, the inside shines slippy like Whitby jet, the sound of water running echoes in the hole. He lowers Hadaway in the keep net, then swings his legs over, checking the rubber inner tube is tight on his shoulder. He moves his weight until he's sliding on his belly, dropping to catch the edge with his hands. His feet find purchase. Letting go, he stands shining the torch, every surface hard and black, a rusted pickaxe sticks from a wall that sparkles like tarmac.

Simon is in a coal mine.

24

RED RIVER RUN RED

Hadaway stands in the net, the game piece glows on his collar like an awful eye looming in the Mariana Trench. Simon places his piece of Big Boy under Hadaway's nose again and releases the ferret from the keep net. Hadaway rushes off, dragging the elastic, the torch beam seeks its white fur. Under foot, a flow of water runs over the coal seam. The golf ball elastic stretches taught, flicking water up as Hadaway searches for the other half of Big Boy. The elastic snaps with a twanging sound, flying back into Simon's face. He runs after the trailing piece, a small hole appears ahead, the elastic zips through it and disappears. Simon puts his face up to the hole.

"Squeaky! If you can hear me, hold on."

He stops to listen to a faint noise. Simon pushes his head in the hole, he takes his penknife and carves into the coal, scraping until he can get his shoulders through. He squeezes and begins a slide that turns into a roll, a hard bounce pushes him into a mid-air fall, the torch is knocked from his hand and it rattles away into the abyss.

Simon lands, huffs, winded. Fighting for a breath he feels movement alongside, guts pounding into his mouth, body wet with sweat and underground water. Hadaway's glowing coin appears then disappears a few feet from him. He shuffles toward the dim green glow; he can see what looks like the outline of a worm. He sidles closer, lowers his head, it's a bony finger attached to the hand he held before they snared the hare over by the train tracks.

"Steven, Squeaky, it's me, Simon,"

No response, Squeaky's crumpled form is hard to make out. The glow of the coin has faded, like people are made of moments, time running alongside. Simon reaches to hold his hand, a lump that must be Big Boy is in Squeaky's palm.

'Do as your told,' comes the sleeping bag voice.

'Is he alive?' Simon asks the voice.

Squeaky's hand is cold like secondhand bath water.

'Go down to get out,' orders the scratchy female voice.

Simon waves the doorstep honey sandwich under Squeaky's nose, Squeaky stirs, breaks into a coughing fit.

"You're alive!"

"Of course, I'm still a bairn, man."

"What happened after Rubba's hand grenade? You've been down here for two whole days."

"I ran to the light, then everything was dark, I fell asleep and every time I woke, it was dark, time filled with quickening, like a hundred lives were all mine."

"Finish the sandwich, Squeaky. Drink some too."

Squeaky inhales the doorstep bread with honey and Simon hands him the bottle of Barley Water.

"We've got to go down to get out."

25

EYES GLUED SHUT

Simon reaches into his haversack, Hadaway is sniffing, still committed to the job. Simon throws a glowing coin forward, it tumbles away, swallowed into nothing.

'To go down you have to go up,' says the voice.

"That's the opposite of what you just said," replies Simon.

"Who are you talking to, Radda?"

"I think it's someone we already met."

"I'm drifting into all the moments, after, before."

"Firedamp gas, Squeaky, that's what we were told when the tekka drew the curtains at school."

Simon turns to look behind. The coin on Hadaway's collar floats up the coal seam behind them, then heads into the silent blackness in front. Simon stands and reaches forward. He can feel a metal bar, then another after it.

"Monkey bars, like Ally Park."

"Are you going to swing it?" asks Squeaky, voice croaky.

"Stand behind me, pull the inner tube over your head, put one arm through, slide it down your back. You'll be safe." Squeaky attaches himself to Simon with the makeshift rubber harness.

"Hold tight."

Simon grabs the metal bar then swings, praying to the God of Legs that there's more, and he grabs each one in turn, swinging heavy. Hadaway's coin bobs, then drops. Simon strains to keep pace, Squeaky's legs are wrapped like broken pipe cleaners round his waist, the sinews in his wrists stretch, knuckles cracking. Hadaway's coin glows down below, Simon releases his grip and they drop to the hard floor. A beam shines from a crack, illuminating stone stairs rising to the light source. Simon carries Squeaky toward the light, the steps glisten as Squeaky takes the first step, kneecaps shining like button mushrooms in the slit. Halfway up the steps a waft of fresh air brings belief in their chances of escaping. Simon looks back to the bottom of the stairs, a yellow canary is preening its feathers on the bottom step. Anne appears next to the bird, floating like Jane, she's dressed in a white hospital gown, holding a child in swaddling. The baby is still, eyes closed, face peaceful.

'Help me with the stairs, please, love,' the mouth of the vision moves with the words, the whisper echoes on the wall on the inside. Simon trips on the step and slips, grabbing at Squeaky for balance, they fall into the dark to the side of the stone stairs. Holding hands they twist, screaming in time, landing with a sickly thud on a pile of dried sticks. Simon and Squeaky banged their heads together, stars swirl in Simon's eyes, he leans back, placing his hand behind his back. He feels a tube-like shape, he moves his hand along, there's a button, it's the torch he dropped from high. He presses the button, the torch flickers, in the flash, two skulls appear like the fox in his bedroom.

He remembers the door vibrating in the cinema toilets, how he looked like a ghost in the reflection. The crop circle and the moments. Squeaky falling asleep, living a hundred times over. The New Town was built to forget, make fresh starts. Squeaky wails, Simon smacks the torch with the hand that punched Lenny, the batteries spring to life. Yellow light floods, skeleton hands hold broken lamps, spread out washed in on an underground tide. The bones saved Simon and Squeaky, broke their fall. For every large skull, a small skull lies alongside, fingers intertwined, the skeletons were cuddling and that's how they died. Animal ribs and what looks like the skull of a pony lies on its side. The poem from school rattles out in front of the squirrel in Simon's mind.

Oh father, 'til the shaft is rid,
Close, close beside me keep,
My eyelids are together glued,
And I-and I must sleep.

'I knew you'd come,' starts the voice from the sleeping bag.

"Are you here now?" asks Simon.

'Up between the cracks, where the sun kisses the earth, we have always spoken, without words, the hare with the crow, the fox and the ladybird, the stickleback, and the mud minnow. You meant well, now the spirits know intentions, it is this that made the words flow.'

Squeaky lies still in the broken coal. The faltering torch reaches to the slit of light, Simon picks his marra up and carries him, the sound of rushing water rises with each step. Hadaway stands on hindlegs, sniffing at the crack in the seam. Simon lifts himself up and takes to the edges with his penknife, the black forest shatters, chunks of devil's gold fall, the thudding wakes Squeaky.

"Pull it out with me, Squeaky, if we can make it wider, we'll get out, get home, start things a new."

A big block drops and they crawl through into another drainage tunnel, Hadaway waits, pink eyes staring at the light at the tunnel's end. They crouch and crawl, peaking filthy faces over the edge, hanging three foot up over a river, the river running red.

"It's blood, Radda, from the skeletons."

"It's dye from the nylon factory, Squeaky, my dad's trying to stop them doing it."

"Let's find a way back to your house, your dad knows how to fix things," says Squeaky.

"Have you not got a dad?"

"Somebody wants to know who I am."

"You can tell me when we get back to the New Town. Now we have to go up and then we have to go down," says Simon, nodding downwards.

"We can put things back together like Big Boy, make it work," says Squeaky.

"Conker Boys, forever."

Simon slips the rubber inner tube from his shoulder, takes the pump from the haversack, connects it to the valve and starts pumping. They share the job between them until the inner tube bulges, standing fat and high. Simon pokes his head round the rim of the tunnel and looks back toward the shore, twenty yards back. The river slides under the pipe, hushed and deep. Simon holds the rim with one hand and hugs the inflated inner tube with the other.

"Do you love your mum?" says Simon.

"Some people took her on the day we went to the slag heap, before I ended up in there," says Squeaky pointing into the dark.

"The same people that bother your grandad when he's been poaching in Presto?"

"I came back from school and the house didn't smell of smoke, my grandad was out too."

"I will be here, Squeaky, wherever you go."

"I'm not going anywhere, Radda."

"Is your half still in your pocket?"

Squeaky takes out his half of Big Boy, Simon brings his half in line, the pieces fit, water drips from the conker. Hadaway's pink eyes stare.

"This is what it's like being brothers," says Squeaky.

"Keep me close, my friend," says Simon.

Squeaky and Hadaway cling to Simon's shoulder, push off from the drainage tunnel into the river. Hugging the rubber inner tube they drift into the middle; cold water greets their dangling legs.

"Do you believe in the God from school?" asks Simon.

"Do you?" asks Squeaky and Simon looks into his marra's brown eyes, face blackened with coal.

"I don't know," Simon looks away as he answers, feeling stupid, thinking of his mum, the version of her that appeared at the bottom of the stone steps, the baby all still that made her ill. Down inside he knows that if he didn't do his chores, his selfishness would make the pain carry on. Little hopeful hammers rage against his homemade wall.

"Do you think we'll ever get a skateboard?" Squeaky's question saves Simon's squirrel from spiraling out of control.

"It's a long time 'til Santa comes down the fireplace wall."

"Skateboards cost too much anyway, for boys like us, maybe not for you but I'm from the old part of a New Town."

"Maybe if we pray, while everything is falling apart, the God from school will listen and give us what we want," says Simon.

"Give it a go."

"Dear God in the cloud, the one with the big finger, not the God of Legs, who is local, please believe us when we tell you that we didn't want to kill the Seaburn Batlads, they wanted to sting us where they shouldn't and things went wrong from there. Rubba didn't know that his hand grenade was real, just like Squeaky didn't know that Tiny the baby leveret was a witch until it died and started talking to my sister. I've been trying harder with my chores so my mum doesn't need to use the wheelchair. We promise you, that we'll forget that we saw the skeletons and the things you allowed to happen in the mine. So, in return, can you please make sure we get a skateboard? Not each, just one skateboard for all of us, it's called a Grentec Coyote, the board is blue and the wheels are ruby red. Please understand, we are not greedy boys."

"And we mean no harm, we just want to cruise the cycle track on the New Town," nods Squeaky.

"Yeah, we don't want to hurt people, we just want to have fun, you must have been young once, even if it was a long time ago," says Simon.

"God's been around for four hundred years, at least."

"We kept our two pieces of a conker for a long time, too."

"Ten months." Squeaky fans out all his digits and offers them to the sky.

"Do you think that will work?"

"Probably, praying for a skateboard, its the right thing to do, when the chips are down."

Hadaway stands straight on the curve of the rubber inner tube. The trees on the riverbank slip past like walking lumber, it's probably Plessey Woods thinks

Simon. On Sundays they'd come here and watch the
trout suck flies from the surface of the water, they'd play
poo sticks on the bridge too. The sun is getting lower,
beams of light break between the trees, water boatmen
skate a merry dance around the inner tube. The dye
from the Brentford Nylons factory has faded, the water is
crystal clear, the surface smells of eel skin. Simon caught
an eel here last year. Cousin Malcolm told him to place
it in a cross scraped in the ground. Simon put the eel's
back into the crack and it stopped writhing. Malcolm
said fish freeze when they get religion. Simon couldn't
get the smell of the eel from his hands and Anne told
him to wash them hard three times. It only went away
when he washed them with a lemon.

"Do you think your mum loves you?" asks Simon.
The words land like flies get caught in open mouths.

"I think my mam's been in trouble."

"The spirits? Or the Babycham?"

"People trouble, she says."

"Like how?"

"There's a green and yellow star jumper down the
back of the sofa like the ones we saw in the tent. She says
a man thinks I'm his,"

"Everyone one wears star jumpers, Squeaky, even the
Bay City Rollers."

"These people are closer, they started it."

"Which people?"

Hadaway's pink eyes glow in the dappled sunlight, the ferret lurches, striking teeth into the inner tube, tearing it, falling apart, black strips of banana sinking in a whirlpool, away to meet the riverbed.

"I can't swim," Squeaky grabs for Simon.

"No one took you to the baths to learn, it's OK," Simon cups his chin with one hand and treads water with the other. He reaches with his free hand, slips his trousers off, pulling them to the surface.

"Tie a knot in the legs and hand them back to me,"

Squeaky uses his free hands to tie the pantlegs. Simon blows into the waist gathered into his fist. The trousers inflate like the chimneys standing tall over Blyth.

"There's a bend coming." They pass a weeping willow and Simon grabs an overhanging branch.

"Hadaway's gone," says Squeaky.

"What do we tell Rubba?"

"That his ferret tried to kill us," says Squeaky.

"Hadaway saved us and the voice from the sleeping bag was helping."

"I hope it's at the bottom of the river."

"Had your gob, Squeaky, wish bad and the spirits come back bad."

The banks of the river are lined with broken rocks of basalt, stained green with algae. A seagull glides, screeching its time-warped horn, the air heavy, salt ready on the tongue, shore crabs below, peeling under every stone. Simon can hear a chorus of voices over the water.

"We know that!" barks Squeaky.

Deep voices roll out 'The Keel Row', the words echo between the river's banks, a song they sang at nursery, when you never know what it was for.

'O wha's like my Johnnie,
Sae leish, sae blithe, sae bonnie?
He's foremost 'mang the mony
Keel lads o' coaly Tyne.'

They clamber the rocks, head for the singing, squelching across the gravel of the car park, toward a sandstone building. Gold lettering spells The Melton Constable. Beyond the road, the tops of sand dunes puncture the blue sky, the voices are coming from inside the pub. They push the heavy wood door of the main entrance. The inside smells like Squeaky's mam. Simon asks the barman if he can use the phone behind the bar. One quizzical look at their blackened faces and he hands the phone over. Simon sticks his index finger in the rotary disk, pulling at the numbers, round and down, six times, the numbers Anne made into a merry rhyme. Seven, one, five, seven, six, six, a pause then a click. The phone rings in the curved plastic earpiece.

"I've been in the river, dad, it's turned red again, we got stuck in the tunnels by the slag heap. Don't say anything, Rubba might get sent to Borstal."

The barman overhears and gives the boys a glass of water.

"Miners drank here, you can join them too."

Simon recognizes the balding man who came to school to talk about the monument at New Hartley, he who read the poem, when the kids laughed. Simon won't laugh at people's pain. He keeps enough of it behind the wall, where the squirrel sleeps the same. The man is buying drinks, the glasses are racked up like ancient amber, humans trapped outside. Simon approaches, catches his eye.

"I saw them down there."

"Where are you from, son?"

"Kramlin."

"We have a memorial drink, a sing song every year."

"The teacher at school wouldn't tell me if they got out."

"Some folk had family you know," he says, pointing back to the room where the singing comes from.

"My friend too."

"What's your marra's name?"

"Steven Squire, but we call him Squeaky 'cos he fell off a Chopper and he can't say some words right."

"Two hundred and four, rest in the ground at Earsdon."

"Not all of them were buried, that kid Lenny was right," says Simon.

"Took many weeks but every man and child were recovered, in good time."

"They didn't finish and I've seen them, where the tunnel comes out into the river," says Squeaky.

"Don't be silly."

"People who leave too soon will talk loud and clear, if you are ready to listen," says Simon.

"What do you mean, bonny lad?"

"Listen to what's inside."

LIBRARY

Today the Queen comes to Kramlin to open Concordia, a new sports center with a fake wave machine. Everyone is excited, apart from Simon. Squeaky didn't show for the last day of school. The summer holidays are here and Simon still wants a Grentec Coyote skateboard for the Conker boys to share. Kids can drift apart over the summer; school glue loosens and falls away. Simon plans to walk to Squeaky's over the holidays, as many days as he can.

The pupils are gathered on the banks of grass lining the road leading to Concordia, the teacher hands plastic union jacks into sweaty pink hands. Simon sees Keks in the crowd, eyes hunting. Yesterday lunch time, Brassa the spoon controller told Simon that Keks thinks the Conker Boys stole a trophy from his gorse camp. The thought of Keks knowing what's in Simon's sock drawer sends a tingling sensation through his arms. If Keks thinks the gorse camp and the trophy are his, what else is upside down? Simon got used to the whispers and

words in his head but people can't see each other's
thoughts yet. Outside worlds want to collide,
playgrounds hide their dangers, like coal mines or the
fish that wage war on man.

With Squeaky off school he's going to miss the
Queen's visit to Kramlin. Her Royal Highness was wiped
clean from the penny by the Inter City train, now the
memory of her visit won't belong in Squeaky's head.
Experiences get stolen like money, like life taken from
baby skeletons cuddling in the mine. Children need
their parents badly and boys should help at home, all of
the time. Growing up is a slow avalanche, big pieces can
hurt but if you don't swim, you don't fly.

Rover, Hillman, Morris, Austin the boys would stand
in the roundabout by Presto, shouting at the cars. The
Rolls Royce screams 'born with money', the rest will roll
the way the wind blows them. The Queen sits in the
back, a posh shop dummy, dressed in teal, looking like
playdough.

"Show us your crown," shouts Keks moving closer to
Simon, flecks of spit clearing a path through the flapping
children. The Queen waves her arm back and forth like a
sprinkler, side to side the gloved hand glides. The
council watered the grass against regulations, everything
is bright and green this time. Children thrash flags like

over enthusiastic swordsmen swatting flies. Presto has been shut for the morning, Squeaky's grandad would have to go without the packets of mash potato he passes between pocket and hand. Simon heard that Squeaky's mam was taken away by people from the council. Keks used to say Squeaky's dad died, Rubba said he was in prison. Boys in Borstal get inky tears scratched into their faces next to their eyes, you can't escape all the things that happen, no matter how hard you try.

Keks swings a punch aimed at Simon, he swerves, dashing through the flags, running for cover in the library alongside. Keks hisses, "That was my trophy" from behind. Through the double doors, into the toilets Simon rolls. Keks comes in, sets the toilet taps running, smashes the lock off Simon's cubicle, bursts in like a devil hog looking for stolen bairns, Simon leapfrogs over him, scrambling past the hissing water and through to the main library. The snap of Kek's voice punches at the air behind him. Simon dances down through the bookshelves and finds a storeroom and locks the door behind. Keks hovers, rattles away at the handle. Simon waits and watches through a high window. The Queens car is leaving, Keks has given up too, he's outside, crossing the road, raging.

Simon exits the storeroom, the books feel like they are

breathing, holding so much inside. He takes his time to walk softly through all the information and gets a sense of calm inside. When his English teacher read poetry it set his heart on glide, made him feel alive. He sees an unusual set of drawers made of pine about three feet wide. He bends down to read the white tags, the top one reads Maps of the New Town. He pulls the thin heavy drawer out slowly and a detailed drawing of the New Town is laid out inside. He traces his finger up the zig zag path to the golf course and back through the Stickleback Forest to the spine road and back to the St. Nicholas church. He finds the drainage lines, the tunnels they've crawled, all except for a big one, one they've not yet found. At the back of the reservoir, a red line runs by Seg Hill. His finger follows the map, the tunnel passes under Delaval Hall and comes out close to St. Mary's by Collywell Bay between The Melton Constable and The Delaval Arms. He remembers the rocks and cliffs of Charlie's Garden, where the fisherman smacked the cod's head with a priest and the shadow of the pony cast long between rock and sky.

He closes the drawer and looks out the window. All the kids have gone, rushed home to start their six-week holidays. In the library corridor Simon sees a poster for a sea fishing competition, the prize is twenty-five pound. Simon's squirrel holds up a Grentec Coyote in the pleasure centers of his mind. Riding down the hill between the social club and the chip shop would feel special. Would help get Squeaky back, make this summer holiday the very best of times.

Simon heads for Rubba's house on his way back, he kicks a plastic union jack along the cycle track until he sees Rubba's house and knocks on the door.

"Can't believe that school is finally over, Rubba! There's a fishing competition, if we win it, this summer will be the best one we've ever had, we can get Squeaky back, have muckle fun."

Rubba's dad appears behind Rubba.

"Did I just see you kick the union jack down the path, laddie?"

"I was just coming to see Rubba, and thinking about fishing."

"Is this the boy who gave you the scar?"

"He didn't do anything, dad, he's a good lad, Radda."

"If you see a white ferret when you're out menacing, let me or Anthony know, Hadaway they call him, he won't come when he's called."

"Yes, dad," says Rubba.

"I'm off to the social club."

Rubba's dad leaves in a uniform, smelling of moth balls. Rubba waits until he is out of earshot.

"Keks is after us all, Radda, I saw him chasing you past the Queen."

"Brassa reckons he thinks the gorse camp is his and the trophy I've kept in my sock drawer is his too."

"It was the Seaburn Batlads who dug up the leveret and scratched SB in the ground."

"They might have left that shaggy dog note but I reckon it was Sandra and Becky who scratched the message in the ground. Remember they pulled each other's hair out over that trophy after school that time."

"I'm going to take the trophy over to that radgie gadgie then."

"Which gadgie? There's radgies everywhere, man."

"The one we knocked on when you were bleeding in his roses, after your dad's hand grenade blew a hole in the tunnel. I think it's Becky or Sandra's dad."

"We're trying to forget about that hand grenade at home, now."

"Your scar has turned white, it looks good."

"It's easier to like than have."

"If you're not going to come to give the trophy back to the radgie gadgie, will you at least promise to help win the fishing competition?"

"After I've had me tea."

"Shake on it, tea or no tea."

They spit and shake hands. Simon heads back home, slides into the utility room, kicks his shoes off next to the wheelchair and heads up the stairs to pick up the trophy from his sock drawer. Jane meets him halfway, where the box tipped before her tongue was split, then tied.

"When you feel bad, they can tell if you want to do right or wrong, it's the way of the land," says Jane, one eye stuck shut, tongue healed up, lisp gone.

"I'm going to give the trophy back."

"More than the trophy, Simon, there's things on our insides."

"Like what?"

"There'll be signs."

"What's going on, my loves?" says Anne from the lounge as the music from the Onedin Line plays loud.

"Nothing, mum," they answer, in their different ways.

Simon runs in his room and opens his sock drawer. The trophy rolls back and forth next to the owl egg. He wraps the trophy in a T-shirt and heads back out through the kitchen to the utility room. Peter is spraying a can of WD40 on to rusted metal by the garage in the sunshine.

"Have you seen an inner tube under the caravan, son?"

"I took it to rescue Squeaky, dad."

"Tell me when you take things, son, then things won't have a chance to go wrong."

"I'm sorry, dad."

Simon opens the back gate and heads toward the slag heap with the trophy wrapped under arm. A boy called Richard from the year above rolls past on a new skateboard, the sight of the prize at stake, almost drives Simon mad. The remains of the pram lie in the ditch at the bottom of the manmade hill, wheels buckled, carriage caved in, a brick alongside. The sandstone house he called on to use the phone with Rubba looms large. 1862 gleams on the white block of rock above the door. He knocks the black door three times.

"Who is it?" a gruff voice sounds.

"I've come to say sorry," says Simon.

The door opens.

"I found this trophy in the gorse over by the old oak tree by St. Nicholas church," Simon hands it over.

"You little blighter, why did you steal it then?"

"I didn't steal it, I came here to say that I'm sorry."

"What for?"

"I took your golf balls over by Arcot Hall."

"Grew up some then, rat boy?"

"I'm learning right from wrong, that's all."

"You'll never know the difference."

"What about you mister?"

"Me?"

"You make the river run red and that's a lot worse than anything I've ever done."

As the man slams the door, a Harlequin ladybird lands on Simon's shoulder. He heads for home along the cycle track, a familiar figure appears ahead of him, Squeaky's Grandad Joe.

"Where'd Squeaky go, Joe?"

"Things happened at home."

"I miss him bad, will you let him know?"

"Aye."

"Can you help me, Joe?"

"What is it, son?"

"We want to win the fishing competition, so we can get a skateboard. We need someone to tell us how to fish the sea and lend us the right gear to go."

"Alreet, bonny lad."

"We're after cod."

"Hard in the summer but I can help you. Come to the allotments over the back of the slag heap tomorrow."

BAIT BUCKETS

Anne is sat in the wheelchair in the kitchen. Simon grips the chair's black handles, leans and tips his mother back toward him, the front wheels lift over the step in the utility room.

"Can you take me round to Auntie June's please, love?"

"I did the stairs, mum."

"It might be time to give you some more chores."

"I'm not sure," says Simon with a smile that Anne returns.

Simon walks in the heat to Joe's allotment, a kestrel hovers over the square patch raising plants and the cock-eyed shed leaning to. Joe's boiling a kettle on a gas stove, Simon sits down on a weeding stool.

"First of all, are you sure it's a sea competition, bonny lad?"

"I folded up the poster, it's got everything on."

Joe takes the paper in his muddied hands, unfolds it and reads.

"The comp's boundary is from Newbiggin down to St. Mary's, 10 am to 3 pm, Saturday the 24th of July. Biggest bag wins ten pound, heaviest fish sweeps twenty-five."

"If we win, we're after a Grentec Coyote."

"What you wanting an animal for?"

"It's a skateboard, to ride with Squeaky."

"You won't see Squeaky."

"He's my best friend."

"I know sonna, but some things have to stay behind closed doors."

"I just want to ride a skateboard with him from the social club to the chip shop, just one time."

"Pick that rod up over there in the corner, the two pieces need attaching to each other."

Simon gets the rod and connects the pieces. Joe picks an old wooden reel from the shed wall, two inches thick, its circumference the size of a dinner plate, three holes are cut out of the main body, a brass wing nut holds it to the center and two thimble sized handles turn it round. Joe shows him how to attach the reel to the metal seat of the rod.

"Squeaky wants to learn these things too, he likes engines and my dad."

"I've done what I could do for the bairn, a boy needs to see strength from a man, on the inside."

"Like the fishing line."

"Aye, the Scarborough, the line's strong for the gullies, where you must go, to Charlie's Garden."

"I've been to Collywell Bay before with my dad, I've seen a man catch there."

"Cod lie in the kelp over the summer, turns them red."

"Like the factory does the river. I've never seen such thick line."

"It's rough down at the bottom, son."

"What bait do I need?"

"Fresh crab and mussel, wrapped in sheep's wool, to keep it on in the tide."

"Where do I get those from?"

"I'll get your bait and leave it in a bucket on your step the morning of the competition. You can get the sheep's wool on barbwire fences, between the livestock fields and the New Town."

"If I win and get the skateboard, can we go and see Squeaky, just one more time."

Joe stares at Simon, for a moment he looks like he's going to say something. The kettle comes to the boil and Joe lifts it off the stove.

"You'll need these," he says, handing Simon a heavily laden Presto bag.

"I'll let you know if we win Joe, thank you, you're a good man."

"Never fish the sea alone, bonny lad."

"Rubba's coming but he'll have to be back for his tea."

"You all got lucky in that tunnel, son."

"I got Squeaky out, and that makes us brothers now."

"I know, good marras don't come round so many times, I can see why you want him close."

Simon lifts the Presto bag, heavy with lead, hooks and rigs, throws it over his right shoulder, rests the reel and the rod on the other and heads for home. On arrival, he places the fishing gear down on the concrete floor of the garage, Peter is alone inside.

"I need to get sheep's wool to keep the bait on, dad."

"Where did you get that from?"

"Squeaky's grandad, Joe."

"He's been in trouble with the water authority last week, taking salmon, without a license."

"Please don't make bad things happen."

"I'll have a word, let them know he helped at the works with the fox that time. Come on we'll drive to the works, there's sheep kept on all four sides."

The Hillman Hunter makes a knocking sound as they pull up to the fence between the water works and the fields. Sheep's wool hangs in the breeze on the barbed wire.

"The tappets need looking at, son."

"You normally fix everything."

"The car's going into the garage on Saturday."

"I was hoping you could take us to the fishing competition, dad."

"I need to get it fixed to go to hospital with mum. How about your friend's parents, son?"

"Rubba's dad likes to wear army uniforms."

"What do you mean?"

"He doesn't do things with his son."

28

TAKE A LITTLE TRIP WITH ME

Saturday, July 24, 8 am 29 degrees.

Peter took the car into the garage early then took Anne to the hospital; the kids are at home on their own. Simon answers a knock at the door. A bucket filled with seaweed sits on the top step, Joe must have been and gone. Simon bends to move the seaweed to the side with his fingers, green crabs scuttle across the freshly pulled mussel. He goes into the garage, collects the fishing gear, puts it in the utility room and waits for Rubba to knock on. Rubba arrives, limping.

"I twisted my ankle in the crack by the caravan, I can't walk far."

"Go round the back, I'll meet you."

Simon collects the fishing gear and opens the gate, rests the rod up against the fence.

"Watch these, and hang on."

Simon goes into the utility room and takes the wheelchair onto the paving stones. Jane's face appears in his bedroom window, she's holding the owl egg and the clay pipe with the child's face and nodding slowly.

Simon pushes the wheelchair out in to the cul de sac.

"Ride in this Rubba, I've got a plan."

Down the zig zag path Simon pushes Rubba in the wheelchair, rod rested on his shoulder, bait bucket, torch and loaded Presto bag on Rubba's lap.

"The coast is miles, Radda."

"I saw a map in the library."

"What kind of map?"

"The map they built the New Town from."

For the first time since May, the sky has dark clouds, as black as the coal the skeletons were digging up down the mine.

29

BIG ONE BY THE REZZY

Hotter Than Ever

Simon pushes Rubba down the zig zag path, across the spine road and up to the hole in the fence by the reservoir.

"How you going to get the wheelchair over?"

"Go in first and I'll pass you the reel with the line."

Rubba crawls under.

"Take the line off the reel, hold one end then throw the reel over to me again."

Rubba throws it over and Simon wraps the line from the reel around the handles of the wheelchair. Simon crawls, joins Rubba and they start pulling the wheelchair over the fence.

"To the big one, let's go."

"I'll get scared going back in a tunnel, Radda, after last time."

"We've got everything we need to win the fishing competition. Do you want the Conker Boys to have a skateboard, or not?"

"Don't leave me like Squeaky."

"We didn't leave Squeaky, we needed to get your head sorted on the outside, you have to do the right thing on the inside, one thing at a time."

They ride the wheelchair across the empty reservoir, hundreds of fish lie dead in the dried-out mud. A plum tree by the entrance of the tunnel holds its fruit, they're all dusty and dark purple now.

"From here to Charlie's Garden."

"The Conker Boys ride!"

"I felt something on my cheek, Radda."

"It's the first time it's rained since the voice in the sleeping bag."

30

MISSED BITES

"Rest the torch on top of the Presto bag, the tunnel is big enough to stand and push inside."

Simon pushes them in.

"It's comfortable, Radda."

"Better than the last one, aye."

The crabs scurry over the mussel in the bucket. The scratchy sound scares them at first, then it becomes normal and they continue the ride.

"I reckon we are about a mile in, there'll be a side tunnel, then two more, then we'll be facing the sea, ready to fish the competition."

"Radda, look down."

The black clouds that sat by the Cheviots have opened up on the cracks in the land. A small stream of water gathers pace round their feet.

"We better get going."

Simon increases the pace, thighs burning. Pushing Rubba feels like a helpful betrayal, cutting guilt right down the middle, adding more to the other side. If his mother needs the wheelchair when she gets back from hospital then no number of chores would fix the way that could break him inside. But Rubba needs the wheelchair to help them win the competition, they will use the prize money to get a Grentec Coyote, share it to get Squeaky back, and around the cycle tracks they would ride.

The water is up to Simon's knees, pushing like it's coming down a water slide.

"We're going to drown, Radda."

"Up front, there's daylight, we're here. Collywell Bay and Charlie's Garden is out on the other side."

The tunnel ends, opens out, the sea is calm in front , all around the shore, jagged rocks eat the water and the sky. Simon folds the wheelchair and props it up against the tunnel.

"Where d'you reckon the fish are?"

"Joe said in the gullies, but the bottom is rough and the tide will take the bait if we don't wrap the sheep's wool on tight."

The boys clamber across the rocks to the deepest gully, the tide is low, it's hard to tell which way the water's going.

"Let's set up next to that big rock at the side."

"But there's hardly any water in the gully."

"I reckon we should stick to what Joe told."

They sit down next to the big rock and Simon threads the thick line from the reel through the eyes of the rod and pulls it down next to the bulging Presto bag. He reaches in, ties a rig with a big hook to the end of the line and attaches a heavy lead weight with granny knots. The crabs move in the bucket, he chickens out of wrapping one on. He splits a mussel with his knife, scoops out the orange insides and threads it onto the hook. Reaching into his pocket he pulls a pluck of sheep's wool and wraps it round the mussel. The wooden Scarborough looks like a wheel stolen from a medieval pram, he lifts the rod and holds the wooden circle still with his index finger, making sure the line doesn't run. With a deep breath he shuffles to the edge of the gully.

"Careful, Radda, it looks slippy."

Simon flicks the tip of the rod gently and releases his finger from the reel. The rig spins round and flies back toward Rubba, landing in the kelp by his hand.

"That could've hooked me, man!"

Simon tries again, this time the rig and weight arc high, landing with a satisfying sploosh in the middle of the gully. The tide is rising, the water dark, almost oily, the kelp floats in welcome of the dipping from the incoming tide. Time passes like in Stickleback Forest, with a rod like this, Simon could be mistaken for a man.

"Why aren't the fish biting?" asks Rubba.

"Good things take time."

"Come on, check it, there could be something on the end."

"It's on the bottom with the sheep's wool keeping the bait on."

"It's been out too long, I reckon."

Simon gives in to Rubba's impatience and lifts the rod to reel in. The tip bends hard, Simon tries pulling the rod up, reel finger clamping the Scarborough down. The line pings, tension gone, and it drops down onto the water. Simon reels the slack in, the rig snapped off at the swivel.

"You've got to leave it in until you get a bite, it's rough on the bottom, it will snap the line unless there's a fish on," says Simon.

"How does that work?"

"The fish swim you up and away, I don't know, we can ask Joe, next time."

"Look, your mother's wheelchair."

"Where is it?"

Simon puts the rod down and runs back across the rocks to the entrance of the tunnel. The rainwater has

washed the wheelchair between a crack in the rocks.
Simon climbs down, grabs a handle, tries pulling, it's
wedged in hard. The barnacles cut his fingers; a little
blood drops on the ground.

"We're stuck here, Rubba."

"Every time we go in those tunnels, the doo doo hits
the fan."

"What do you want to do then?"

"Keep fishing, that's what Conker Boys do when
times get hard," says Rubba.

"Good lad."

Simon loads the hook up with mussel and casts a new
rig smack in the middle of the gully, bulging with fresh
salt water brought by the blossoming tide.

The rod tip knocks like a cat whacks its paw on a rat.
Simon lifts, it feels different this time, a movement of
weight like a loaded conversation pulls you down. He
turns the Scarborough's wooden handle round;
something down there wants to steal his line. Tugging,
nodding, strength growing all the time.

"Hold my waist, Rubba, something big's on."

Rubba sidles up, holds his chest from behind. The
rod is bending, juddering, fighting the imposition,
whatever's down there is using its weight against the tide.
Simon holds firm, sinews straining.

"It's like the man on the boat in Jaws, I saw you go to the toilet that second time."

"Thanks for not telling,"

"Thanks for stopping me from going to Borstal, like my brother, and not dibbing on my dad."

"I thought Squeaky had died, I didn't say at the time."

"Where is Squeaky now?"

"Joe said some things that have to stay on the inside, the fish is getting tired, hold the rod, I'm going down."

Simon slides down to the edge of the gully, a white belly glows under the water by the side. Simon pulls the line, the belly gets bigger, a huge mouth appears, brown spots on red flanks shine in the summer bright light. He slides two fingers under the gills and manages to slide the fish out of the water onto the rocks. A cod, pushing fifteen pounds, rests on the kelp like a white bellied ghost dragged up from underground.

"My god, Radda! We're going to win the competition."

A pony on the cliff top casts it's shadow on the rocks of Charlie's Garden, Simon looks up in its direction. Feelings spill over his squirrel as he looks into the fish's eyes. The eyes of the leveret swap back and forth with the gold in the cod's eyes. He reaches his hand into the giant mouth, removes the hook, and slides her back into the water, tail kicking, the fish swims away in the slowing tide.

"What are you doing man, Radda! That was our skateboard you just let go."

"I don't want any more guilt, if you let it build up, it gets harder to hide."

31

CAREFUL WHAT YOU WISH FOR

Someone up on the cliffs must have seen the boys on the rocks, or maybe the police just happened to be passing by. The wheelchair got washed away into the sea at high tide. Simon was practicing what to say in the back of the police car. The truth was best, even though it seemed hard, things got better when you told the truth. Lies grew like rumours and darkened like mold in the mind. The police dropped Rubba off first, Simon could tell Rubba's dad was used to seeing cars with lights on top, there was something dead in his eyes. Simon managed to keep Joe's fishing gear, although it was hard persuading the policeman to let him put a dirty bucket in the boot of the car.

The police are pulling into the cul de sac to drop Simon off and the Hillman Hunter is missing in the drive. Simon opens the gate and puts the fishing gear in the back garden and knocks on the utility room door. There's no answer, it leads him to the front door, he presses the bell. Jane comes to the door holding a plastic Pony.

"I've been combing it's hair, you should try," she says.

"Is it a new toy?"

"Yes."

"Where's mummy?"

"They came and then they went out again."

"Is she in the hospital?"

"Where do you want her to go?"

"To come here, to come home."

Through the kitchen window the back gate opens. Peter has a box in his hands, Anne follows, helped by the support of two walking sticks. Simon runs to greet them, ready for the truth to be told.

"We've got a little something for you, son."

"Mum, I've been bad."

"We got you a present to help with what's going on with your mum."

Peter hands Simon the box.

"I have to tell you something."

"It can wait for a minute, son, go on."

Simon opens the box by the vegetable patch, the red wheels of a Grentec Coyote appear from the wrapping, glowing like round chunky rubies in the sun.

"We've known for a while that you've wanted a real one."

"I took your wheelchair to the sea and I lost it, mum."

32

SCOTLAND BOUND

Peter made Simon fill in a property loss report for the hospital and he was docked pocket money, until it matched the cost of the wheelchair. Even though Anne's was free on the NHS. Peter explained the hospital would have to buy a new one. Ten pounds was a lot of money, but penny for the guy was coming and the Conker Boys could use teamwork to pay for one. Anne didn't use a wheelchair anymore. She was getting better and used a walking stick when her knees started to play up.

After the dust settled, Simon decided to ride the new skateboard over to Squeaky's house. The wheels felt smooth on the cycle track, time disappeared again like it did in the crop circle or when the forest stream whispered into nothing. When he got there, Squeaky's house felt different to look at, peering through the lounge window, the walls were bare, no brass horseshoes, no furniture, just a worn-out carpet on the cottage floor. The interior of the house looked like he felt on the inside, his shared friendship, gutted, gone.

He looked down at the skateboard and sighed, the chance to share a ride past the social club to the chip shop had flown.

Placing the blue plastic deck down on the path outside Squeaky's house he pushed off, tried to smile, it wouldn't come. The path was bumpy here and the ruby red wheels rattled against the imposition of the rough ground. He skated past Presto on the cycle track and headed for the zig zag path and the cul de sac. Picking up the Grentec Coyote he crossed over the road onto the roundabout. A red Rover begins its approach like the Queen's Rolls Royce did, the shaven headed driver looks like the man who swam butterfly in Blyth. Lenny is sat in the front seat picking his nose. On the back seat is the girl who drove the motorbike at the gorse camp and the slag heap, next to her is Squeaky.

When worlds collide, your breath gets stolen, puts your guts into your mouth, sends shivers down your sides. Simon can't help himself as the car passes over the roundabout and he sets off after the car shouting "Squeaky!" as loud as he can. Billy stops the Rover, Simon catches up with the car, like those inside caught Squeaky and tried to sting them with nettles in the tent before they caught the leveret that died. Lenny rolls the window down.

"Where are you going?" asks Simon, breathless after the run.

"Scotland, but I'll still get you back for smashing my trumpet, ya little maggot," comes the reply through green-tinged teeth.

"I'm sorry about what happened to your trumpet, Lenny. Give this to Squeaky, if you can," said Simon, handing the skateboard through the window. Lenny takes the board from Simon's shaking hands and Billy from the swimming baths puts his foot down.

Simon stands waving as Squeaky looks on glum through the back window. The Rover runs away, dips with the road and then disappears, like Paul who used to live next door did. Simon feels blank like an empty moment, the weight of the nothingness stops him crying. Squeaky belonged with the Seaburn Batlads, and with that he gained Billy as his real dad, a brother in Lenny and a sister in Sookie. How could Simon be sad?

Simon still wasn't sure about what happened to Squeaky's mam. Like Joe said, some things should stay on the inside. Simon understands now, wanting good things for people felt better than wanting them for yourself. He started to learn that from his mum and dad but his friends helped him finish the idea, because friends teach you to love. Trying not to be selfish takes a lifetime to master, and the longer it takes us, the more you get to feel sad.

VOICE NOTIFICATIONS

Sometime near now.

Simon was reaching for a memory, something for his old grey squirrel to hold after bad times. The fan on his Mac laptop is whirring, it's been hot outside. eBay notifications for a Grentec Coyote have been arriving in his inbox. Nostalgia fills like bath water; it only stays warm for a while. Simon lives down south like the people who used to talk on the radio. Tunbridge Wells to be precise. Peter's still up north in Kramlin, getting old teaches you to keep your friends, count your blessings, grow wise. Giving is better than receiving, and learning to live through others is life's greatest prize.

It's a Saturday morning in July when the notification for a Grentec Coyote for sale in Aberdeen arrives. The sellers name on eBay reads, 1976Squire.

Simon writes him a message asking if the ruby red wheels glow in the sunlight and the answer comes back, Whye aye!

Simon is up in Kramlin to see his father. He mentions it in a message to 1976Squire who replies, So am I!

They meet in Northumberlandia, a feature park made from rock excavated from local ground, Blagdon and Banks shaped her into a woman and she rises laid down. Simon parks up by The Snowy Owl, walks the forest to a field at the side. A long-haired pony stands next to the barbed wire.

'What took you so long, bonny lad?'

"You were the voice all those years ago in the sleeping bag."

'Galla is the girl in the dark, that's what they called us, with you, I used to work alongside. Between the cracks and the slag heap we formed bonds that never die. Children who learn to love nature and live for others, we will be with you forever, on the inside. Squeaky's up top waiting, it was with his old family that I first died.'

Simon turns to look up at the peak of Northumberlandia, he sees a figure, leaning on the fence that forms a crown round the head of the woman, shaped from the rock dug from the ground. He picks some fresh grass, turns to drop it over the barbed wire fence for the pony, she's disappeared like a stickleback darting, all that's left is a warm feeling inside.

Up top the men look at each other, faces flooding with unforced smiles. They hug and look down at the open cast mine.

"Still gannin' on, Squeaky."

"Digging down deep, on the inside."

"Did you keep your half of Big Boy?"

"I kept it in a drawer in our first place in Scotland, then we moved again and I left it behind."

"I was sad when you left, Steven, and I buried that feeling for a long time."

"Who would have thought we'd meet again where we first learned to survive?" says Squeaky.

"What are you up to now?"

"I'm an engineer, I took the inspiration from your dad."

"He'd be glad to hear that. What happened to Lenny and Sookie, and your dad?"

"Lenny's still naughty, I see him now and again, when the visiting times allow. I lost touch with Sookie but I still have my dad."

"I was happy you got your dad."

"Did your mam get out of the wheelchair?"

"I'll tell you that story another time."

Simon reaches in his pocket and takes out his half of Big Boy.

"Always keep me close, my friend."

"Meet me by the old oak tree," Squeaky replies.

"Let's have that one last ride," says Simon.

THE END

ALL SONGS WRITTEN AND PRODUCED BY THE AUTHOR.

ALBUM MIXED BY ERIK MILES AT PRINCES STREET. ADDITIONAL WORK UNDERTAKEN AT FORUM RECORDING STUDIOS, TUNBRIDGE WELLS.

THE CONKER BOYS AND MOVED AWAY, ADDITIONAL WRITING - STEVE WOODS.

THE HAND GRENADE, ADDITIONAL WRITING – MARKUS HOLLER.

LEAD VOCALS & HARMONY- THE AUTHOR & STEVE WOODS.

DRUMS & PERCUSSION PLAYED AND RECORDED BY- DANNY WARD IN THE MOODYCAVE, MANCHESTER.

GUITAR ON ALL TRACKS- MARKUS HOLLER.

HORN & STRING ARRANGEMENTS, TRUMPET & FLUGELHORN ON THE SEABURN BATLADS, MOVED AWAY & THE HAND GRENADE- RORY SIMMONS, RECORDED AT MANDARAX MUSIC STUDIOS.

VIOLIN & CELLO ON HIGH & LOW AND THE PLACE I CALL MY HOME- ELLIE FAGG & NATALIE ROZARIO, RECORDED BY RORY SIMMONS.

BASS ON HIGH & LOW AND FRIENDS TEACH YOU RECORDED AND PLAYED BY – LANCE THOMAS AT THE PENTHOUSE STUDIO, LIVERPOOL.

SAXOPHONE AND CLARINET ON NEW TOWN SOULS, THE HAND GRENADE AND RUBBER INNER TUBE- JON SHENOY.

TROMBONE ON THE HAND GRENADE, MOVED AWAY & THE SEABURN BATLADS- TREVOR MIRES.

ADDITIONAL HORN EDITING ON MOVED AWAY ERIK MILES.

ALL OTHER INSTRUMENTS – THE AUTHOR.

BACKING VOCALS ON NEW TOWN SOULS, HIGH & LOW & MOVED AWAY ANGIE ALLGOOD.

BACKING VOCALS ON RUBBER INNER TUBE, THE HAND GRENADE, THE CONKER BOYS & THE PLACE I CALL MY HOME, HEIDI HASWELL, COURTESY OF MUCKY PUP.

BACKING VOCALS ON THE SEABURN BATLADS, THE CONKER BOYS AND FRIENDS TEACH YOU- VOX POP MALE CHOIR, STEVE WOODS, REG MARDEN, ELLIOT McCARTHY, MARC CARPENTER, STEVE BARTON, STEVE LEGGE, DEAN NICHOLLS, CHRISTIAN HARRIS.

ADDITIONAL VOCALS ON THE CONKER BOYS -HENRY JAMES RAE
BACKING VOCALS ON FRIENDS TEACH YOU-OSCAR DOERNTE.
BACKING VOCALS ON THE HAND GRENADE-BEN LARKHAM.
BACKING VOCALS ON THE SEABURN BATLADS-MARKUS HOLLER.
BACKING VOCALS ON HIGH & LOW, THE CONKER BOYS AND FRIENDS
    TEACH YOU VOX POP CHOIR, TUNBRIDE WELLS.
STEVE WOODS' VOX POP CHOIR TUNBRIDGE WELLS, GIRLS- JENNY
    GRAHAM, CAROL NAVIS, CAROLYN HUNTER, CAROLINE ANGELL,
    KIRSTY HOSKINS, CLAUDINE CERRINI, JILL MAY, SUSAN NORVILL,
    EMMA BUTTERWORTH, RUTH DASCOMBE, SONIA WHITEWOOD, JO
    PEARSON, SARAH BARKER, MICHELLE CARPENTER, SARAH WEST,
    ELEANOR HUGHES, VANESSA LACEY, HELEN BISHOP, MICHELLE CFAS,
    JO VIDLER, DEE LULHAM, ALICE QUINTANA, CARMEN D, LORRAINE
    KELLY, TINA MANGAR.
VOX POP CHOIR RECORDED BY ERIK MILES IN THE FORUM BASEMENT,
    THE SUSSEX ARMS, TUNBRIDGE WELLS.
A&R ASSISTANCE-PAUL FRADGELY, AMINE RAMER, RICHIE HUME, WALT,
    JULIE & MILO DOERNTE, ANTONY DALY, KATE ROGERS, BEN MORRIS,
    ED PITT, TOM STINGEMORE, ALI LITTLE, IAIN COOKE, DAVE STONE,
    SIMON ARMSTRONG, DANNY WARD, DUNSTAN KESSELER, BEN
    LARKHAM, TOM RAE, CHRIS STRINGER, PETER STEEL, SIMON KILBY,
    CHRIS RABY, IAN HOWELL, MARK PICKSTONE & BRIAN MAUGHAN.
THANK YOU TO THE CARPENTERS FOR THE INTRO TO THE CHOIR.
COVER ART AND BOOK DRAWINGS-HENRY JAMES RAE.
THANKS TO JORDAN VADNAIS & RYAN HARTIGAN.
THANK YOU TO ALL THE STAFF AT CLAREMONT PRIMARY SCHOOL,
    TUNBRIDGE WELLS.
THANKS TO STEVE WOODS AND VOX POP CHOIR.
DESIGN - PAUL ARNOT
    MASTERED BY - KEVIN TUFFY, MANMADE MASTERING, BERLIN
MUSIC DISTRIBUTION - BEN MORRIS, KUDOS, LONDON.
P&C MARK'S MUSIC 2024

Side 1

NEW TOWN SOULS

It's hot outside, are you ready for a story from a long, long
time ago?

Verse 1

Staying in on a Sunday, all the shops are closed
Praying for shiny fun days, when the grass gets mowed
We went to town to see a film, about a shark who kills for fun
We didn't say inside too long, we were scared of the
monster's song

Chorus

I feel alive, I feel alive, the revelations here
My heart is young, my world is small
I'm learning what to fear

Verse 2

Playing in cardboard boxes, by the Presto store
Praying we'll live for ever; we don't ask for anymore
We learned to be the best of friends, stay together to the end
No one knows what the future holds, it don't add up when
your ten years old

Chorus repeat

When they tell you to love God, does he know you exist?
Will he help you with your chores? It hasn't rained for a
long time; do you think about the cracks in the ground?
You don't remember and you don't recall, we ruled a world
that was oh so small
We closed the door on that special place, forget my name
but never forget my face

Chorus repeat

Outro

Feeling fine cos I'm living on a New Town, feel alive cos I'm
    living on a New Town
Drink lemonade from the back of the pop van, Sherbet Dib
    Dabs in the family caravan.

I WISH I HAD A SKATEBOARD

Verse 1

I wish we had enough money, to ride four wheels like in the
    magazines
Being young is not funny, trying to realise all your favourite
    dreams
Ladybirds up in the sky, lazy Sunday passing by
Long lean, holiday dream, we will fly

Chorus

I wish I had a skateboard, to roll around the town
I wanna ride a skateboard, and cruise across the ground

Verse 2

I tried to keep a pet bunny, but it ended bad, by the tree
And motorbikes, they sound funny, better hide your toys
    from the killer bees
Ladybirds up in the sky, lazy Sunday passing by
Long lean, holiday dream, we will fly

Chorus repeat

Wish I had a skateboard, wanna ride a skateboard

THE SEABURN BATLADS

Ohhh, it's the Seaburn Batlads they'll have you
It's the Seaburn boys on a roll
It's the Seaburn Batlads they'll have you
It's the Seaburn boys

Verse 1

Aaaayeeeahhh
See this hammer, feel this fist, see the slag heap, see the
    mist
Hear this trumpet, taste the spit, looking for trouble? Can't
    handle it
We dug up your rabbit, burned your camp, smashed that
    bogie, snapped that ramp
Stole your skateboard, broke the wheels, boys mean
    business, how's that feel?
I divvent confuse and I don't forget, the nettles in the tent
    when you punched me neck
Said you've got an army, don't know what for, listen to the
    trumpet, this means war
In the ground the ghosts are found, and they're coming out
    to play

Chorus repeat

Verse 2

See these nettles, feel this heat, see the train tracks, hear
    the beat
Shaggy dog stories never complete, ghosts in the mineshaft,
    baby feet
We move like maggots, dress like tramps, crash your
    parties, lick your stamps
Steal your pushbike, slash the wheels, boys mean
    business, how's that feel?

I divvent confuse and I don't forget, the nettles in the tent
    when you punched me neck
Said you've got an army, don't know what for, listen to the
    trumpet, this means war
In the ground the ghosts are found, and they're coming out
    to play

Chorus repeat

It's ghost time, give it to them Lenny, underground style
Yuh knaa what happens when you mess around with the
    Seaburn Batlads, ha ha

Chorus repeat

THE CONKER BOYS

Wait for me, by the old oak tree

Verse 1

We climb the trees, we live, and we grow
We scratch our knees, in the tunnel we must go
When I hear that rumblin' sound, Inter City London bound
I say that I pray that, you can be found

Chorus

Always keep me close my friend
Meet me by the old oak tree
Always keep me close my friend
Find the time
We can share a conker, to the end
Find the time to play

We dance with bees; we swim and row
We fish the seas, in the tunnel we must go

When I hear that tumblin' sound, Inter City Scotland bound
I say that I pray that, you can be found

Chorus repeat

Ahh ah, we are the conker boys
Ahh ah, we are the army boys

Chorus repeat

Outro

Row the keel row, we'll row the keel row
Row the keel row, we'll row the keel row
Wish't! Lads, haad yer gobs, Aan aa'll tell ya aall an aaful
    story
Gell la jalla eek aa laa

HIGH & LOW

I'll be searching high & low
To find out where the love goes
I've been searching high & low, high & low

Verse 1

If there is a god up in the sky
Can you ask him the reason why?
You put my people through so much pain
Is this what you want? Is this part of the game?
You've got me asking so many questions, and I'd really like
    to know
I wanna know where it goes, so he really knows, I love you
    so

Chorus

I'll be searching high & low
To find out where the love goes
I've been searching high & low, high & low
When I find it, he'll take away your pain
Make you smile, we'll walk together again
I'll keep on searching, high & low

Verse 2

At the bottom of the stairs, I saw you cry
Something inside me just wanted to die
But I'm just a young boy, still selfish in my ways
I will learn to care for others, through the memory of your
pain
You've got me asking so many questions, and I'd really like
to know
I wanna know where it goes, so he really knows, I love you
so

Chorus repeat

I would like to pose the question, where does all the loving
really go?
Tell him I need to know, tell him she needs to know

THE PLACE I CALL MY HOME

Verse 1

All the kids play games in the cul de sacs, in this brand-new
world, in our anoraks
But it's down below, where the tunnels go, where the water
would, if the water flowed
In the morning, we can climb down, underground to the sea
In the morning we'll be fine now, come roll with me

So many souls are crying, it echoes down the walls
Somebody's babies dying, to the sound of waterfalls

Chorus

Through the tunnels we will roam, where the ghosts are set
    in stone
To the place I call my home

Verse 2

All the kids write names on their haversacks, in this brand-
    new world, there's no looking back
To the fox the crow, from the stream the flow, to the
    stickleback and the mud minnow
In the morning, we can climb down, underground to the sea
In the morning we'll be fine now, come roll with me
So many souls are crying, it echoes down the walls
Somebody's babies dying, to the sound of waterfalls

Chorus repeat

'Cos the bricks are in your soul, yeah, the bricks are in your
    soul

Chorus repeat

THE HAND GRENADE

Verse 1

They call you Rubba Knees, I know, and you like a little
    escapade
We all do crazy things for show, but no one needs a hand
    grenade
Please don't pull the pin, I don't wanna end up in the bin
Please don't pull the pin, (I'm fallin' in) this is the world I want
    to be living in

Daddy was a soldier, mummies not home
What you gonna tell them on the telephone?

Chorus

My friend, he's stuck in a tunnel, Rubba blew it up now were
    all in trouble
We need to find a way home, gotta find a way home

Verse 2

They call you hard to please, I know, and life is just a big
    charade
We all do crazy things for sure, so come and join the
    masquerade
Please don't pull the pin, (I'm fallin' in) I don't wanna end up
    in the bin
Please don't pull the pin, (I'm fallin' in) this is the world I want
    to be living in
Daddy was a soldier, mummies not home
What you gonna tell them on the telephone?

Chorus repeat x 2

Squeaky knows where the mash potato goes, yeah he
    knows, he knows

Chorus repeat

Find a way home, find a way home, I'm fallin in, I'm fallin in
And I don't wanna say goodbye

RUBBER INNER TUBE

Verse 1

Take a little trip with me, ride until we find the sea
Fresh water meets salt water, tiny drops of rain
You'll feel no pain
Let the current take you down, lazy river wipe this frown
Let the water take you down, ooh, ooh, ooh

Chorus

Floating on a rubber inner tube
Feel your body floating
Floating 'til you just can't feel no more
Gliding on a rubber inner tube
Floating 'til you just can't feel

Verse 2

Take a little dip with me, into blue water where the fish swim
    free
Fresh water meets salt water, tiny drops of rain
You'll feel no pain
Let the current take you down, lazy river wipe this frown
Let the water take you down, ooh, ooh, ooh

Chorus repeat

And we'll be holding on, 'til our day is done
We'll find the fun, in the midday sun

Chorus repeat

You don't have to build a wall, let the rain drops fall
Just you and me, on the river down to the sea

MOVED AWAY

Intro

It's breaking my heart, breaking my heart, now you've
    moved away

Verse 1

I didn't wanna let you go but something in my heart told me
    you know
I gotta face the truth, sometime
Boys don't always tell each other how they feel
You can miss somebody, and the feeling's real
Don't wanna move on, tears are hard to conceal

Chorus

It's breaking my heart, now it's breaking my, it's breaking my
    heart, now it's breaking my
It's breaking my heart now you've moved away
 It's breaking my heart
Now you've moved away

Verse 2

I was feeling guilty, head was low, sometimes you've got to
    grow
'Cos the road is long, and the road is tough, and this, you
    already know
Boys don't always tell each other how they feel
You can miss somebody, and the feeling's real
Don't wanna move on, tears are hard to conceal

Chorus repeat + If only you could stay

Don't want to lose a friend again, feels bad, just
    remembering

You were the best friend I ever had, when you left it made
   me so sad
Gonna miss you (movin' on, you're movin' on)
Gonna miss you bad (movin' on, you're moving on)

Chorus repeat + If only you could stay

Time is moving on keep those bonds real strong
You don't know how long we get to stay

FRIENDS TEACH YOU

Verse 1

Yes, I know that things aren't good at home
You're a hungry boy on this road
And you should know that you'll never be alone
Be alone, my friend, listen to me

Chorus

No matter where you go (no matter where you go)
I will be right here for you (I'll be right here for you)
I won't be scared to show (friends teach you to love)
I'll always be here for you (friends teach you to love)

Verse 2

With you I'm learning, with you I grow
With you I'm turning, with you I show
Yes, I know that things have not been good at home
'Cos your mummy drinks Babycham, oh no
And you should know that you'll never be alone
Be alone, my friend, listen to me

Chorus repeat

With you I walk, with you I run
With you I talk, with you
Friends give you the reasons, how to love
Squeaky, are you still down there? Squeaky, hold on
Do do's
They say there's witches and the spirits live down below

Chorus repeat

I'm gonna be here for you
From the old to the new, if the love is true, if you move away,
    I'll come back to you
Friends give you the reasons, how to love